A Bloodtrail Through the Dirt Roads of Mexico...

Carter came over the last heap of rocks right into a hornet's nest. He had already unlimbered the shotgun, so that by the time he hit the rise both guns were firing.

There were three of them, two outside the car and one, the driver, trying to move it.

The first one tried to bring his Stechkin into play, but froze when he saw the man hurtling down at him from the rocks. Instead of the Stechkin in his right hand he threw his left up imploringly.

The first slug hit him in the armpit, came out his shoulder, and embedded itself in his neck. The impact flopped him over onto his belly and the second shot went in his back, skidding him half a foot farther. A third bullet severed his spinal column, leaving him to twitch and bounce on the ground like a squirming worm on a hook. He screamed, knowing he was going to die...and anxious to get it over with!

NICK CARTER IS IT!

FROM THE NICK CARTER
KILLMASTER SERIES

COUNTDOWN TO ARMAGEDDON

KILL MASTER

NICK CARTER

J

JOVE BOOKS, NEW YORK

KILLMASTER # 243: COUNTDOWN TO ARMAGEDDON

A Jove Book / published by arrangement with
The Condé Nast Publications, Inc.

PRINTING HISTORY
Jove edition / November 1988

ISBN: 0-515-09806-X

Jove Books are published by The Berkley Publishing Group,
200 Madison Avenue, New York, New York 10016.
The name "JOVE" and the "J" logo
are trademarks belonging to Jove Publications, Inc.

PRINTED IN THE UNITED STATES OF AMERICA

10 9 8 7 6 5 4 3 2 1

*Dedicated to the men of the
Secret Services of the
United States of America*

ONE

The Mexican sun, high now, burned through a slit in the drapes and fell across the bed. Nick Carter blinked once and then came awake like a cat. The eyes opened and remained open, the senses of sight and smell and hearing orienting him in that first instant.

He was in the posh apartment of Alexandra Dragos. The apartment was above a private club called Cerrio's. The club was near Embassy Row, in the south of Mexico City across from the university. It catered to wealthy businessmen, tourists, and most of the embassy crowd.

Alexandra Dragos had run the club with an iron hand for the past ten years. For eight of those years, she had also moonlighted for the CIA and the American State Department. A private club like Cerrio's was a good place to have ears when diplomats from fifteen or sixteen countries were letting their hair down.

Carter had worked with Alexandra Dragos before. They were old friends, old enough friends that, within two hours after arriving ten days earlier in Mexico City, Carter was in her bed.

Beside him, Carter heard her even breathing and felt her warm, naked flesh fitted to his back. Reluctantly, he disengaged himself and rolled to the edge of the bed. When his bare feet hit the thick carpet, he reached toward the night table and his cigarettes. He lit one and moved silently to the window.

Ten days. Ten days of sleeping with a beautiful woman and tending bar in a posh lounge. Ten days of waiting for something that might never happen.

It was part of his job, the waiting, but N3, the top Killmaster for supersecret AXE, still didn't like it.

David Hawk, head of AXE, had put it to Carter in no uncertain terms two weeks earlier, in Washington, D.C.

"Mayflower has been turned for eight years, Nick. He's been a good agent, first in Moscow, then Rome, and now Mexico City. As a top cipher clerk for the Rome and Mexico City embassies, he's been invaluable."

But now Mayflower felt as if his string was coming to an end. He wanted out, so he had called "uncle."

Carter, because of his familiarity with Mexico—and his relationship with Alexandra Dragos—had been chosen to bring Mayflower safely back to Washington.

"There is one hitch," Hawk had continued. "They know they've got a hot one . . . they just don't know who it is. They also know he's about to run. So there may be problems."

The "problems" Hawk referred to were, of course, the necessity to terminate anyone who got in the way of moving Mayflower to the United States.

That was another reason for the choice of Nick Carter as the mover. He was the Killmaster, an expert at termination.

"Needless to say, Mayflower will stuff everything he can in his head before he runs. We know they have a couple of big projects in the fire that Mayflower is privy to. That makes a safe move all the more important."

The original contact, the "got to go" word from Mayflower, had come through the same channel in Mexico City who had been relaying his intelligence, Alexandra Dragos.

There was one rub: *nobody* knew who Mayflower was. That had been part of the deal when the Russian had first contacted a CIA operative in Moscow. It was all sight unseen.

And there was the risk for Carter. What if Mayflower had already been blown? They could pawn off a plant, and the Killmaster wouldn't be the wiser until it was too late.

It was almost noon, time for Carter to go below and open up the bar. That was his cover, day bartender for Cerrio's.

He returned to the bed, crushed out the cigarette, and leaned against the headboard.

She sensed the heat of his body and, even in her sleep, turned toward him. He reached, found the woman's thigh, and squeezed lightly. There was a change in the way she breathed. It became deeper, more abrupt. Without waking, she groped for his hand and guided it higher.

Carter smiled to himself, pulled his hand away, and shook her shoulder. Alexandra Dragos sighed and came awake, slowly. Her eyelids fluttered. She saw him at the edge of the bed, a lean, dark shape.

"Morning," he said.

She made a purr in her throat and moved her hand over the washboard ridges of muscle in his stomach. "It's early."

"It's noon. I have to go to work."

"Shit."

She rolled up on one elbow. Soft red hair feathered out from her head and she combed it back with her other hand, yawning, showing good teeth.

Alexandra Dragos had good everything . . . sultry dark eyes, soft olive skin, and a compact body with full breasts and hips.

"Today might be the day," she said.

"Let's hope so."

She made a face. "Then you'll go and I won't see you for another two years."

The Killmaster's tanned, craggy face broke into a smile. "Alex, you'll never want for playmates."

She returned the grin and ran her tongue over his ear. "I'm getting too old for quantity," she said, her eyes twinkling. "Quality interests me more."

Her hand moved between Carter's legs and he tried to ignore it. "In two years of contacts, it's still amazing that you've never met Mayflower."

She shrugged and fondled. "Not really. He's afraid. He's uncovered two moles in your agencies."

"Are you sure it's a *he?* There are nine people in the code area of the Soviet embassy. Three of them are women."

The hand stopped. The rounded shoulders gave a little shrug, making her bare breasts come alive. "I don't think so. If Mayflower were a woman, I would know it."

"I suppose," Carter sighed, and made a move to rise.

She pulled him back and leaned across him, mashing her full breasts against the corded muscles of his arm. "Pedro can open up. I'm the boss, and I say you can be a half hour late."

Her scent reached him. He drank it in, filling his lungs with it. She was moving over him now, and his vision filled with the inviting hollow of her cheeks, the fullness of her lips, the perfection of her shoulders, and the glory of her breasts.

She looked at him, her lips slightly parted. He reached and fondled her breasts, taking one in each hand and gently cupping them. She pushed her chest against his kneading fingers and moaned softly.

Carter turned her beneath him and covered her body with his. His lips fell on hers, just a brush of his tongue at first, but it was enough to bring a moan of desire from her throat.

"You can be late," she whispered.

"Maybe a whole hour," he replied growling as he moved between her legs.

It was just after four. The office crowd was filling in, lining up at the bar. They would drink until six. Then the married ones would go home to their wives and husbands. The single ones, those that hadn't already scored, would go on the hunt.

Carter was behind the bar with the other barman, Pedro. Alexandra was moving from table to table, pumping up business. The two cocktail waitresses were being efficient, serving drinks and avoiding grabs as they moved through the tables. The piped music was Mexican, the chatter of conversation international, at least eight languages.

The Killmaster spotted him the minute he lumbered through the door. He was stocky, swarthy, with a mane of wild black hair combed back from his forehead with his fingers. He was dressed in a mussed suit with too much lapel for the current style, a shirt with too much color and ring around the collar and a stained necktie with too much knot.

He had a sullen mouth and dead eyes. He also had an ugly scar from behind his right ear that ran down his throat and disappeared under his dirty collar.

His name was Gripon Malenkov. Originally he was Bulgarian, but Moscow had long ago recognized his talents and brought him into the KGB.

Malenkov liked to kill people. He enjoyed it. He'd gotten the scar on his neck four years before on a boat. The boat had been on the Danube, near Budapest, and he had been trying to kill two agents, one American, a man, one MI6, English, a woman.

He had succeeded with the woman, mutilating her in the

process. He had failed with the man. That's how he had gotten the scar. There were two more scars on his chest where Carter had tried to bury his stiletto, Hugo, in the man's heart and failed.

Just inside the door, Malenkov paused, his eyes scanning the room. When he saw Carter, he stared. The thick salt-and-pepper brows came together, but the Killmaster sensed that no connection had been made.

Of course, then, in Budapest, Carter hadn't been sporting a droopy Zapata-style mustache, heavy sideburns, and slightly tinted eyeglasses. His hair had been long then. Now it was a neat brush cut.

The change was enough to block Malenkov's instant recognition, but Carter knew that it would be only a matter of time before the Bugarian's thick head would sift through its memory bank and remember.

Carter turned from the room and polished a glass. He watched the stocky man in the back bar mirror. Malenkov moved through the crowded room like a well-coordinated bull, and took a dark, corner table with his back to the wall.

The waitress, a buxom young thing in a costume that emphasized a lot of the top of her front and the bottom of her rear, moved to the table. Malenkov ordered without seeing her. His eyes were working the room.

Was he in Cerrio's because he knew it was a contact place? Carter wondered.

Or was he just working the street?

One thing was for sure. If Malenkov was in Mexico City and prowling, it meant only one thing: stop the runner. In this case the runner was Mayflower. And, for the Killmaster, that meant stop Malenkov.

The girl gave Pedro the order, a small draft beer.

Carter grinned. It wasn't that Malenkov didn't drink. It

was more that the KGB didn't give its operatives crap for expense money. More than one KGB operative had been blown by such a silly thing. It just wasn't good form to go into a place like, for instance, Maxim's in Paris and order a beer. Carter had seen it more than once.

He waited, watching in the tinted mirror behind the bar as the girl delivered the drink. When he was sure Malenkov had temporarily forgotten him, he moved down the bar to Pedro.

The Killmaster was already figuring. It wouldn't be much of a chore to have Malenkov snuffed and buried in one of the huge dump sites just outside the city. There were bad boys in poverty-stricken Mexico who would do that little item for a few hundred American dollars.

No good.

The Mexico City *rezident,* Malenkov's boss, would figure what was up, and simply send someone else. Carter knew he might not spot that someone else until it was too late.

Pedro had lots of brothers. Two of them ran a fish distributing outfit in the Yondo Barrio.

"Pedro," Carter said from the side of his mouth, "are your brothers busy tonight?"

The thin shoulders shrugged and the face remained expressionless. But the eyes lit up. "Depends."

"On what?"

"Money, of course."

"Of course," Carter said dryly. "See the mean one with the scar, over there in the corner?"

Pedro nodded. "Looks like a very unhappy man."

"I'd like to make him even more unhappy. It's an old score."

Pedro would not question the request or the reason for it. He knew Carter was more than a bartender, and he knew his beautiful boss did more than push booze. But he couldn't care less. He made *mucho* pesos, and there were many chances for little bonus envelopes like the one Carter was offering. In Pedro's family, they all shared the work and the wealth.

"What will you need?"

"The delivery truck, and one of your brothers to drive, for starters."

"Any hands on?"

Carter shook his head. "No, he's mine. They just drive the truck, with him in the back, to the plant. Then they cut up some fish or something while I use the garbage room."

"Sounds good. How much?"

"Five's a nice round figure."

"When?"

"About an hour."

Pedro moved off down the bar toward the telephone.

He stood in front of the open file cabinets under a bank of pale yellow lamps. One by one he lifted the file folders, examined them, and dropped them back into the drawer.

He was tall, well dressed, with an athletic physique, wide at the shoulder and narrow at the hip. His face under the curly black hair was handsome, more Mediterranean than Slavic. Many of his co-workers, usually the women, often wondered why he had not chosen a career in film instead of going into government service.

His name was Viktor Prokudin, and he was first assistant to the KGB *resident* in Mexico City, Oleg Grechko. His contacts in the American CIA and the State Department knew him as Mayflower, and they would have been delighted to know that he was not just a cipher clerk but a man in a position of power.

"What do you do with all the information you collect, Viktor?"

Her voice, from the doorway behind him, held a harsh echoing quality in the huge room.

Prokudin didn't move at once. He stood still, sliding the file drawer shut quietly. Then he curved his full, sensuous lips into a smile and turned.

"Amalia, darling, you dressed quickly, and you look radiant."

She stood, hipshot in the doorway, the crimson slash of her mouth curled in an odd smile. She was dressed in a skintight black sheath that emphasized every curve of her voluptuous body. A full-length fur coat was draped over one shoulder, held by a thumb. A tall glass of vodka was held shakily in her other hand.

She looked young for fifty. Her body was firm, the skin like antique ivory, and the breasts high, two sexual invitations rather than glands for suckling the young. Not that they had ever been put to the test. Amalia Grechko had refused to have children. She adored her body too much to have it stretched out of shape in the birthing process.

"Where do you sell your information, Viktor?"

He took a few tentative steps in her direction. "Amalia, more of your wild ideas . . ."

She laughed. "You mean my drunken delusions, don't you?"

As usual, she was drunk. Not falling-down drunk, but very close, as she let the fur coat slip to the floor and lurched from his grasp.

"I warned you, Viktor. I want to be loved, not used."

Prokudin built the façade of adoration back into his face and moved in behind her. Gently, he slipped his arms around her and cupped her breasts.

"I have loved you for nine years, Amalia."

Again she laughed and struggled from his grasp. "You've screwed me for nine years, Viktor, and in the process screwed my husband, the party, and your motherland."

"Amalia . . ."

"Oleg suspects. I've warned you, Viktor, but you wouldn't stop. When I first guessed what you were doing, I didn't care. All I cared about was your magnificent body. Well, no more. If you fall, Viktor, I won't go down with you. Now drive me to the banquet as you've been told to do."

She still had her back to him, and simultaneously two thoughts went through Prokudin's mind.

The first was that she was very attractive, sleek-looking and beautiful, even from behind. With her rich blond hair falling loosely to the base of her neck and the lines of her body clearly stated in the second skin of her dress, she could, even now, arouse him.

The second thought that struck him was that she would have to die. He couldn't afford to wait two more days to give the signal. He would have to do it tonight. He would try one more time at the embassy compound to find the name before he ran.

But first he would have to kill Amalia Grechko.

She finished the glass of vodka as she turned, then stood swaying, one hand on her hip.

"What the hell are we waiting for?"

"Nothing," he said, and picked up the fur coat.

He had trouble getting her down the stairs and across the courtyard, but he finally achieved it. Outside in the warm moonlit night, he led her, staggering, to the Volvo limousine.

Evidently her final decision to betray him, coupled with

the huge amount of vodka she had consumed, had taken all the spine out of her body.

"Pity," she said, her spittle spraying him. "You had a brilliant future, Viktor."

Not anything like the future I'll have with my freedom, a new identity, and the more than two million American dollars they have already paid me.

"Amalia, my dear, you are drunk and irrational."

He opened the door, but assisting her in was no easy matter. He heaved, tugged and pushed until she was finally sitting in the passenger seat.

"I should be in the back," she said, slurring her words. "What if they see me in the front with the chauffeur when we arrive at the restaurant? Ish bad form..."

He slammed the door without a reply. Moving around the car to the driver's side, he looked up at the sky and shuddered. Years ago, he knew this night would come. Now that it was here, he hoped he could go through with it.

He moved past the car, back toward the rear door of the mansion.

"Where are you going?"

He patted his pockets. "I forgot the keys."

Inside, he went directly to the phone in the study, the only one in the house that didn't have a recorder attached to it. That had been Amalia's idea so that they could agree on the times and places for their illicit liaisons. Many times the clean phone had come in handy for him.

He closed his eyes in concentration for a full minute, recalling the two numbers. One of them he had dialed almost weekly in the last year. That was the number that signaled the woman that he was making a drop. The second number was the signal that he was coming out. It would be the first time he had ever dialed that number.

He focused and dialed.

Over four miles away, in a residential section of north Mexico City, one of two telephones rang in a small, one-room flat above a meat market.

The telephone was attached to a relay device. It clicked, and Prokudin said one word: *"Da."*

There was another click and the line went dead. The machine would automatically dial the woman's private line in her apartment above Cerrio's.

Now everything was in motion. Prokudin hung up the phone and headed for the door. As he passed the bar, he grabbed a bottle of vodka.

He was pretty sure he would need it.

TWO

Pedro replaced the receiver on the wall phone and headed back down the bar toward Carter. He spoke in passing, "My brother, Angel, will be outside the rear exit in fifteen minutes."

Carter finished the drink order, rang it up, and removed his apron. He went through the kitchen and up the rear stairs. He rapped once on the door to let Alexandra know it was him, and entered.

She was on the bed watching television, dressed in only a sheer bra and panties. She started to smile when she saw him stripping off his white shirt.

"Again, so soon? Nick, you're an animal."

The smile disappeared as he went on by the bed to the dresser. "Can you get dressed? It's not too busy, but Pedro might need a hand if it fills up."

"What is it?"

"Problems," Carter replied, strapping a spring-release chamois sheath to his right forearm and slipping the stiletto he called Hugo into it.

Alexandra rolled instantly from the bed and stood. "What kind of problems?"

Quickly, he related the background on Gripon Malenkov, and his own guesses about the Bulgarian's sudden appearance. As he spoke, he pulled on a black turtleneck sweater. "He didn't recognize me at once, but it's only a

13

matter of time with me down there behind the bar, until he does."

She was slipping into a functional skirt and blouse to work behind the bar. He was attaching a silencer to the snout of a 9mm Luger. This done and a fresh clip in place, he slipped it under his belt in the small of his back.

"Is that necessary?" she asked.

"It might be. Maybe not. What I want is information. He's not here to enjoy the sunshine. I want to know what the real reason is—"

Carter was interrupted by the ringing of the phone on her bedside stand.

"Sí?"

From clear across the room, even with the phone pressed to her ear, Carter could hear the recorded music coming through the instrument. She listened for only a minute, and hung up.

"He's coming out . . . tonight."

"You're sure?" Carter said.

She nodded. "That's the signal. If it's a drop, it's Beethoven. That was Prokofiev. No maybes: he's coming out tonight."

Grim-faced, Carter headed for the stairs and Gripon Malenkov.

Prokudin opened the driver's-side door of the Volvo and saw that Amalia was asleep. Her head was back against the seat and her mouth sagged open. She was snoringly asleep.

He started the car, turned in the wide drive, and headed for the white brick pillars. Just as he passed through and turned right toward the northern mountains, he took a snort from the vodka bottle.

He drove until the lights of the city were far behind him. The bottle was nearly empty, about three fingers left. He upended it on the front of Amalia's dress and threw it out.

Ahead, the powerful beams guided him. He was coming up on a crossroad. To the left, a paved four-lane road led to the lower shelf of Lake Texcoco. To the right, a dirt roadway led around the lake to the upper shelf.

He turned right.

Beside him, the woman stirred. "I wanna drink."

"Soon."

"I wanna drink . . . now." She came out of her stupor and up into a sitting position. *"Dibashka . . .* where are we?"

He slid his hand up her back until he could curl his fingers in her thick hair.

"What are . . . ?"

Her forehead hit the dash with a dull thud. He let her slump back to the seat and returned his hand to the wheel. It was hard going now, the wheels of the big car literally jumping from rut to rut.

Ahead was the Tapayec Bridge. It was narrow, skimpy, and without guardrails. It spanned one of the feeder streams that flowed at a steep angle down into the lake. The water at this point was not more than eight or nine feet deep, but the stream cascaded along with tremendous power, and the sides and floor were sheer rock. Whatever went into the stream would be carried along into the lake bed, even a ton and a half of automobile.

His heart pummeled and his fingers trembled as he turned the last curve and the nose of the car lifted in a steep climb. He drove slowly, the car bumping along the dirt road. And then the wooden slats of the narrow bridge were reverberating beneath the tires in solemn, hollow sounds.

He was sweating now, the moisture dripping from his face and neck to soak the collar of his shirt.

His toe was barely on the accelerator, moving the car

forward by inches. He spun the wheel to the left, one toe on the brake, easing the movement until the tires were close, perilously close, to the edge of the bridge.

Below, he could hear the rushing water above the hum of the engine. He slid the shift into the "park" position and wiped his palms on his trousers before reaching for the door handle.

Quickly, he got out of the car, slammed the door, and looked in on the woman.

She was still out, sleeping now. The bruise on her forehead was hardly discernible.

He was trembling violently. His mouth was open, drawing in great gasps of air. His clothes were pasted to his body and he could smell the stink of fear he radiated.

"Do it," he hissed to himself in the darkness.

His throat was constricted and his lungs burned. The nape of his neck was rigid as he leaned through the open window and pulled the lever down into "drive."

The car lurched an inch or two, and stopped.

The woman slept.

Prokudin sweated.

He couldn't get back in the car and hit the accelerator. If the car moved forward, he might not have time to dive to safety before it went over.

A rock . . . he could put a rock on the accelerator. . . .

He walked off the bridge and off the road. The only rocks he could find were boulders that he couldn't lift. Cursing, he returned to the rear of the car.

His feet were heavy, as if they were weighted. He barely had room as he leaned his shoulder against the trunk and pushed. The car moved, but not enough. For a fleeting moment he felt that this thing of chrome and steel and glass and rubber was resisting him all on its own.

Then he saw it. One of the rear wheels was wedged

against a plank a little higher than the others, just high enough to block forward movement without power being applied.

"Sonofabitch!" he cried, and summoned up all the force in his frantic body.

He pushed again, this time with a swaying, rocking motion. Slowly, on the third try, the rear tire eased over and the big car moved forward.

From there on it was easy. The car kept moving. The momentum carried it over far enough so that when the undercarriage hit the planks it wasn't enough to stop it.

It teetered, paused, and then flipped over to land on its roof. Immediately, the current caught it, swirling the big car in circles. Then it started down toward the lake, turning on its side and disappearing beneath the surface.

Viktor Prokudin stood shivering in the warm night air on the edge of the bridge, his eyes riveted on the spot where the car had vanished.

Thick ripples of water spread in the center of the stream. He stood there until the ripples abated and the bubbling ceased, until the current flowed evenly again, sparkling in the moonlight down to the lake.

Carter slipped down the narrow hallway past the rest rooms and cracked the rear door of the club. A pair of headlights illuminated the garbage-strewn alley, and the panel truck came to a halt just opposite the door.

Angel stepped from the truck. He was a huge man, twice the size of Pedro, and, in the dim light, looked twice as mean. He opened the rear panel door, looked around and moved lazily back to the driver's seat.

Carter closed the door and walked back down the hall toward the interior of the club.

Malenkov had been careful about choosing a table to

keep his back to the wall, but careless about the proximity of the table to the hallway. Carter had slid into the opposite chair before the man had even see him.

"Hello, Gripon," Carter whispered in Russian.

"Huh . . . ?"

"Budapest, the launch on the Danube, my stiletto. You're a good swimmer, Gripon."

The eyes narrowed and then the bells went off, and what animation was possible in the dark flat face appeared.

He started to come up out of his chair but the snout of the silencer just above his belt buckle settled him back.

"Carter."

"The very same." The man had started to curl his fingers under the edge of the table. "Don't do it. I'll put your spine against the wall in pieces, call it a bar fight, and drag you out before anyone sees the blood."

"What do you want?"

"I question, you answer." Another movement, and Carter put two more inches of the silencer in the man's gut. "What brings you to Mexico City?"

"I work . . . at the embassy."

"You didn't work at the embassy two days ago."

"I move around a lot."

"Yeah," Carter replied, "you do that. Killed any women lately?"

A grimace that passed for a smile split the flat face. "Not lately."

"We're going down that corridor and out the back door. A little chat."

"If I don't?"

"Then I'll shoot you where you sit." Carter lowered the Luger and jammed it into the man's crotch. "Okay?"

A nod, with sweat suddenly popping out on the broad forehead.

"Good. Keep your hands on the table and get up, slow. Walk out the back door. Do it right and you may be able to walk back in."

Gripon Malenkov was a pro. He did exactly as he was told. He knew Carter did not want blood, at least not in a crowded bar. He worked himself away from the table, keeping his hands in sight. Halfway down the darkened hallway, Carter put his face to the wall with a shoulder and kicked his feet wide.

"Move, one move, and your brains are part of the plaster."

With the Luger behind Malenkov's right ear, Carter patted him down. He stood docilely as the Killmaster relieved him of a nasty looking .32 automatic and a switchblade. He also found a tiny .22 in an ankle holster.

"You always go out for a drink this loaded?"

"There is a lot of crime in Mexico."

"You're so right," Carter replied. "Move!"

The Bulgarian walked out the rear door obediently. Carter windmilled his right arm and caught him solid behind the right ear with the butt of the Luger. He went face-down in a puddle of smelly water, and didn't move.

Angel was out of the truck in an instant, hoisting the man up by the armpits. With one heave he sent the stocky body into the rear of the van and slammed the door behind it.

"The plant?"

Carter nodded curtly. "Tie him up in the room where you keep all the guts until it's hauled away. He's mean and tough, so don't take any chances. Also, don't let him see your faces, in case I let him go. I'll be along later."

He watched the panel truck bounce down the alleyway until it was out of sight. Then he turned in the opposite direction and walked two blocks down the alley to an all-night garage. The boozy night clerk barely looked up as the Killmaster walked past his cage.

The lower level of the garage smelled like urine and was lit by only one huge bulb swinging from the high ceiling. He walked directly to a black Trans-Am and unlocked the trunk.

In the trunk was a .30-caliber M-1 sniper rifle with a night scope, a Savage over-and-under shotgun, and a small sack of M-1 grenades. He checked the loads in the guns, separated the spare clips and shotgun shells from the grenades, and closed the trunk.

There was a small workbench in the rear of the garage area. There, he stripped Malenkov's .22, wiped the parts clean, and threw it and the Bulgarian's switchblade into the half-full oil drum. The .32 automatic he stripped as well. Then, using a hammer and small chisel, he chipped away at the firing pin until it was only a nub. This done, he reassembled the gun and jammed the loaded clip back into the butt.

Back at the Trans-Am, he slipped his Luger into a holster strapped to the underside of the front cushion. The .32 went under his belt where the Luger had been.

He brought the engine to life and checked his wallet: three thousand American. Even if he gave a grand to Pedro and the brothers, he still had more than enough to get to the U.S. border.

The powerful engine responded and he glided out to the street. One turn brought him around to the front of Cerrio's. He parked in the No-Parking-Passenger-Unloading slot, and went inside.

Pedro and the part-time bartender were behind the bar. Alexandra must have called the man in, knowing that she had lost Carter's services.

The piano player was taking a break and Alexandra was

having a drink with him. As Carter came in, she swung off the stool at the far end of the bar and walked toward him with that leggy strut he knew so well. The way she carried her body was a sight to behold, enjoyed by every man along the way.

She had changed out of the skirt and blouse. Now she wore a pale silver sheath that molded the long, tapering thighs and reflected the pale lights along the wall.

"Is this it?"

Carter nodded. "Packed and loaded."

She stood close to him, fingers gripping the tight muscles of his upper arm. "It was fun, *amigo.*"

"Until next time."

Her full lips didn't smile and her eyes were a shade too narrow, calculating. Carter, trailing his fingers along the curve of her back, thought she was going to say something.

She didn't. Instead, she pressed close to him and brushed her lips across his. Then she just walked away.

Pedro was by the door. Carter pressed ten hundreds into his hand.

"*Adiós, amigo?*"

"Yeah, *amigo,*" Carter said. "*Adiós* it is."

He pushed through the door and slid into the Trans-Am. Seconds later, with the engine roaring, he was headed toward the mean part of the mean city.

THREE

A ride with a truckload of pigs had brought him back into the outskirts. From there, he had taken a taxi to within a block of the embassy.

Now it was nearly nine o'clock. Figure an hour to the rendezvous. So he had two hours.

He was probably a fool for coming back around the embassy at all, but he had to make one more try for the name. He had the list of those who would be sailing, but not the identity of the one who wouldn't be finishing the voyage. If he could take that name with him to the Americans, there would be very little he could ask for and not get.

Also, he would need to check out one of the embassy cars. He had planned to use the Volvo, until Amalia had come up with her tantrum.

"Viktor, I thought by now you'd be swilling vodka and cramming caviar down your throat!"

The gate guard was named Arkady. He was too old for a foreign post but he was distantly related to someone high in the party. Viktor Prokudin had made it a point since his own posting to go out of his way to make friends with the junior officials. Arkady paid little attention to his comings and goings.

"Comrade Grechko remembered some work that I hadn't done in the code room," Prokudin replied dryly. "You know how that goes."

23

"Da, it is the story of my career."

Prokudin slipped through the crack in the gate and walked across the courtyard to the side door. Inside, another guard waved him on and returned to the newspaper he was reading.

He climbed the wide, sweeping stairway to the second floor and took the secure elevator to the third. Across from the elevator, he punched in his identification number on the digital box by the code room door, and waited until the light blinked green.

The outer room was strictly for collating, evaluation, and reports. Several desks with typewriters on one side and small computer terminals on the other filled the room. Beyond a second steel door was the master code room itself, with the cryptographer machines and the banks of communications gear.

There would be four, perhaps five people on duty in the code room. Here, in the outer office, there was only one duty officer.

Prokudin cursed his luck when he saw who it was.

"Good evening, Comrade Anna Androvna."

"Comrade Prokudin," she hissed through a wreath of cigarette smoke around her graying head. "What do you want?"

Anna Petemkin disliked all men in general, and handsome, playboy types like Viktor Prokudin in particular.

"I need some information for Oleg—"

"At this hour? I thought he was celebrating his wife's birthday in one of those decadent restaurants in the Zona Rosa."

Prokudin shrugged. "You know Oleg. He remembers something he missed and he wants to clarify it at once. I'll need the access code for the computer."

She sighed, making her pendulous breasts heave in the

heavy sweater she habitually wore even in midsummer.

"Very well. What's the file number?"

"Blue . . . K-2, GH001."

The woman nodded. Without speaking, she rose and led the way down the aisle on the left side of the room. Prokudin fell in behind her. She was a short woman, a bit on the heavy side. She wore a dark wool skirt that was too small for her, obviously so from behind. Her shoes were unstylish, practical, thick-soled. The only sound when she walked was the faint *hiss-hiss-hiss* of her heavy nylon-covered thighs rubbing together. The woman stopped at a cabinet in the far left corner of the room. She pulled out a large, flat drawer. It was filled with folded files. She riffled through them, then found one.

She unfolded it before handing it to Prokudin, saying, "I'll just check it."

From a desk to his right, Prokudin gathered a heavy onyx paperweight.

"No, no good," she said, shaking her head vigorously. "This is a *Dronovka* file, Eyes Only for senior officers. Why do you . . . ?"

He hit her behind the left ear, slamming her against the file cabinet. When she kept turning, with her eyes still open, he hit her again, this time in the center of the forehead.

Her soft body made a plopping sound rather than a thud when she hit the tile floor.

He dropped the paperweight and bent to feel her pulse. She was still breathing and her pulse was strong. Every instinct, every cell in his brain, said kill her.

His fingers curled around the thick folds of her throat, but he couldn't do it. Instead, he dragged her to a supply closet and left her there.

Then he returned to the file drawer, found the correct

file, and quickly memorized the access code.

It was 9:17 when he sat down at one of the desks and switched on the computer.

It was a street made up of crumbling two-story build-ings, tiny stucco houses with tin roofs, and out-and-out tar-paper shacks. A few lights burned. Cars, most of them old and on blocks, were parked closely together on both sides of the street.

It was dark, but three streetlights provided yellow patches of light along a broken cement sidewalk.

Carter locked the car and moved toward a side street. An old man reeking of tequila stepped from a darkened doorway.

"Nice car, señor . . . very bad neighborhood . . ."

Carter knew the scam. He fumbled in his pocket and found an American five. He tore it in half and gave the old man one piece.

"If it is not a nice car when I return, I will run over your legs with it three times, old man."

"With my life, señor, I will guard it with my life."

When Carter rapped on the door, he looked back. The old man was leaning against the side of the Trans-Am, a tire iron like a rifle on his shoulder.

The door opened and Carter slipped inside. The smell of fish immediately assaulted his nostrils. Not brine-fresh fish, but fish that had been out of the water for a while and sitting around.

The high-ceilinged front room sported two large refrig-erated cases with dirty glass and a running-water tank for live crab and lobster. Angel led the way across the room. His brother, Gordo, a little deaf-mute with sad eyes and a big smile, stood at a block cutting up a batch of snapper.

His fingers, prying and deftly slicing with an eight-inch blade, fairly flew.

Gordo looked up, saw Carter, and signaled hello with his bloody fingers.

Carter nodded and turned to Angel. "Back there?"

"*Sí.* He came awake while I was wiring him. I had to thump him again."

"Just so he's alive enough to talk," Carter growled.

Both brothers wore wraparound rubber aprons over baggy rubber waders and boots.

Angel saw the look. "You want some gear?"

Carter nodded.

"In the refrigerator. The cold kind of neutralizes the smell when we ain't wearing 'em."

Carter went to the walk-in refrigerator. There were two outfits hanging on meat hooks. He brought down an apron and pants, and found a pair of boots. Two minutes later he emerged dressed.

Once outside, the smell again hit him, forcing him to breathe through his mouth. "God, fish do smell."

"Mostly when they're dead," Angel said with a grin, and joined his brother at the block.

Carter waddled toward the rear room. The smell when he opened the door was ten times worse, overpowering. He stepped inside and reluctantly closed the door behind him.

He felt the soles of the boots slide on the old planks of the floor. The boards were soaked through with fish oil, blood, and scales.

In the center of the room, Malenkov sat in a chair, his wrists bound behind him with wire. He was awake, mean, and very unhappy.

"You will answer to the authorities for this, Carter!"

Carter laughed out loud, and was immediately sorry.

The quick gasp of air had filled his lungs with the putrid odor.

"Bullshit. Gripon. In our business, the 'authority' is the one with the gun. And right now I have the gun."

He produced the .32 he had taken off Malenkov and slid it back into his belt, this time at his belly under the apron.

"What do you want, Carter?"

Carter shrugged. "It's very simple. We know that you know that we've got a mole. You know he's coming out soon. We know that you know. What I want to know is how much your people have on him. What did they tell you to look for, Gripon, when they sent you out?"

Malenkov looked somewhere past Carter. "I am merely a driver at the embassy. I have diplomatic immunity. I—"

Carter hit him in the gut, not hard, just a quick, flicking punch. It was enough to make him gasp. And right after the gasp came a gagging sound as the fetid air entered his body in too big a dose.

"How long do you think you can sit in here breathing the stink of dead fish, Malenkov?"

This brought the eyes wide. His dark complexion had a greenish tinge in the light of a single overhead bulb that swung at the end of a kinked wire. Suddenly he was breathing in shallow gasps.

"I know you," Carter said. "Pain can't hurt you. But I think eight hours in this shit would make you want to die."

"You . . . you wouldn't leave me . . . here, in this . . . for eight hours?"

"You bet your ass I would," Carter rasped.

Malenkov rolled his head up and stared at the Killmaster with dark, malevolent eyes. Carter knew that if their situation were reversed, Malenkov wouldn't hesitate to kill him, and kill him as painfully as possible.

"What do they know about Alexandra Dragos?" Carter

said. "Why did you hit Cerrio's tonight? How much does your *resident* know?"

Malenkov's chunky body strained at the tough wire that bound him to the stout chair. He cursed Carter in Russian and broken English.

Carter whacked him, a good one with the back of his hand across the side of the head.

The salt-and-pepper hair splayed out in a wild mop as the chair crashed over. Malenkov landed in a pool of stagnant water. Fish oil oozed through the water like a liquid snake, and scales floated on top of that.

"What's your assignment, Gripon?"

"Fuck you."

Malenkov arched his neck and tried to roll his face away from the slimy water. Carter put his foot on the side of the man's head and forced his face back in it. Malenkov held his breath as long as he could, but when he could last no longer the gasping breath was soon followed by a gagging, retching sound.

"I won't kill you like this, Malenkov, but I'll make you wish you were dead."

The Bulgarian kept gagging until he vomited, but he wouldn't talk. Finally, Carter yanked the chair upright and set it so that the light glared full in the other man's eyes.

Then the Killmaster came on strong in Russian. Not precise, scholarly Russian, but the language of the streets. The words and phrases he used could only be understood by someone who had either studiously studied the tongue or was born to it.

When Carter had finished defiling Malenkov, his mother, father, sisters, brothers, aunts, uncles, and the family dog, Malenkov grinned his odd leer and spit in Carter's face.

So much, Carter thought, *for this bullshit.*

He had tried ridicule and it hadn't worked. Minor debasement had scored a few points but no cigar. Pain was out. Malenkov was tough. He wouldn't break with a pounding. In his lifetime the man had probably taken more physical abuse than Carter could devise.

Carter left the room. Angel and Gordo were still working at the block, just two men putting in their time.

Angel looked up. "Finished?"

"Hardly started," the Killmaster replied. "I need a handful of innards, no bones."

Angel's knife flashed. He gutted a good-sized fish and flipped the result into Carter's waiting hand.

Holding his hand away from his nose, Carter returned to the rear room. He circled behind Malenkov, slid his free hand in front of the man's jaw, and pressed the nerve under the soft side of the bone.

Malenkov's head came back, the mouth open. Carter brought up the handful of entrails so the man could see them.

"Protein, Gripon."

There was a gagging, sickly scream, but no words. Carter pressed the nerve harder and brought the jiggling mess closer to Malenkov's mouth.

"They are going to interrogate her tonight," the Bulgarian suddenly gasped. "It was supposed to be a party, a birthday party, for Amalia Grechko. She drinks a lot, or acts like she does. They were going to load her drinks... wanted to keep it quiet so only myself, Grechko, and my assistant knew."

"Who's she?" Carter asked.

"You damn well know who she is... your mole, Amalia. Grechko's wife."

Carter let this one roll around. Amalia Grechko. He had filled himself in before leaving Washington on every person connected with the embassy. He didn't think Grechko's drunken wife was Mayflower. But if *they* did, then perhaps the real Mayflower wouldn't have to come out after all.

"What was your assignment?"

"A flyer," Malenkov said, his eyes still staring at the dripping innards in Carter's hand. "The Grechko woman stopped in Cerrio's often to drink in the afternoons."

"Just a flyer, huh?"

Malenkov nodded. "If she happened to run before she was interrogated, I thought I could head her off there." Here, he paused and his eyes moved from Carter's hand to his face. "I was right about Cerrio's, wasn't I? Why else would you be working there?"

There it was. Alexandra was finished as a contact, unless. . . .

Carter met the other man's stare. Malenkov didn't know it, but his deduction about Alexandra, Cerrio's, and Carter's employment there was his death warrant.

He turned Malenkov's head loose and threw the contents of his hand across the room. He walked from the circle of light to a wooden bench where he stripped off the rubber apron and, as if it were an afterthought, set the .32 beside it.

There was a sink at one end of the bench. As Carter washed his hands, he spoke over his shoulder.

"I'm letting you go, Malenkov. I should kill you, but I don't see any reason other than revenge for Budapest, and that's past history. I'll have you driven up into the mountains and dropped off. By the time you get back to the city I'll be gone, and Mayflower will be gone with me."

"Mayflower?"

"The mole. That's the code name." Carter picked up a pair of wire cutters and moved back to the chair. Three snips and Malenkov was free. "Run some water over your wrists to get the circulation back."

The Bulgarian stood, flexing himself on his toes to restore the circulation in his legs. Slowly he took off his coat and shirt, and then he went to the sink and held his hands under the cold water tap, massaging his wrists.

Carter lit a cigarette and watched him. Malenkov was stripped to the waist, a waist heavy with fat. It wasn't flabby fat, but the kind of fat an athlete builds with age, the kind that can absorb a lot of punishment.

Carter would soon find out how much punishment the man could absorb.

The movement was quick, deft. Malenkov turned as if to shrug into his shirt. Instead, he brushed the rubber apron aside and came up with the .32.

"I'm not going into any mountains, Carter, and you're dying."

To the man's surprise, Carter only smiled and dropped the cigarette. It fizzled out on the wet floor.

"I gave you a chance, Gripon. You didn't take it. But I can't say I'm sorry."

Malenkov fired. When the hammer thudded on nothing, he cursed and ejected the clip. When he saw the full clip, he got the picture.

With another curse, he lowered his head and charged, roundhouse swinging his short, muscular arms. He was fast, powerful, competent.

Before Carter's knee came up, Malenkov's fists had jackhammered his ribs half a dozen times. But there was no sense of pain in Carter's body, only purpose on his brain.

As Carter brought his right knee up, he laced his fingers together, caught the back of Malenkov's head, and yanked it down. The knee mashed the wide nose flat and came away red with blood.

Malenkov howled and bored in. He was too close to do much harm, but he was also too close for Carter to work on him. Carter pivoted, stepped back, felt his feet slide in the slime of the floor. Malenkov lunged for him again, but Carter had enough room this time. Fingers stiff, he chopped hard across Malenkov's throat, saw the burly man's eyes bug, saw him gasp for air.

Carter swung a right that landed solidly under the heart. As Malenkov collapsed, he caught his oily hair and held him up. Just long enough to drive the hard right fist between Malenkov's eyes, against the bridge of his nose, into the mouth.

The jawbone broke with a brittle sound and the ruined mouth gushed chunks of teeth in a stream of blood.

Carter let the hair go, and Malenkov fell on his face into the fish filth of the floor.

"Get up, Malenkov, get up!"

The stocky body rolled over. The face was a mess, hamburger, with only the eyes alive as pinpoints in a sea of red.

But the killing desire was still there. He started up slowly, and finished the rise like a striking snake.

Carter caught the kick aimed at his gut. He twisted the foot and jerked. Malenkov howled with pain but managed to flip his weight and break the Killmaster's hold.

Then he was up, staggering but on his feet. Carter faked a kick himself and came in, planting three gut-shuffling punches in the other man's middle. Malenkov gasped for air and went to his knees, his eyes staring up at Carter, waiting.

But Carter didn't come in for the kill. It was then that he realized that Carter *did* mean to kill him, but the American was going to punish him first, beat him down until he willingly gave up life.

Such a degradation was anathema to the trained killer.

He came off the floor howling like the wounded animal he was, his powerful arms and fingers seeking a bear hug around Carter's dancing body. The Killmaster moved to the side, evading easily.

Malenkov whirled, totally disoriented now, blood blurring his vision.

Carter caught him on the arm, floating to his rear, digging a series of vicious punches to the kidneys.

The Bulgarian whirled, focused, and charged again, arms flailing wildly, growling like a wounded bear. Carter grinned, feinted with his right, and smashed a left into Malenkov's snarling mouth. The lips split wide and more blood spurted. Carter stepped in and roundhoused a killing chop to the man's side.

The sharp crack of snapping ribs echoed in the room.

Malenkov was an upright dead man now as he staggered away, holding his side. Carter went after him, driving him around the room, evading his rushes and an occasional wild swing. He smashed lefts and rights into the face until it was an unrecognizable pulp of tissue and blood.

"That's for Budapest, Malenkov."

The man tried to speak, but no words came, only blood gushing from his ruptured mouth.

Carter hooked two hard lefts to the body, driving the man against the bench. Dancing away, his foot slipped and he went down on one knee. Malenkov kicked him in the head, spilling Carter flat on his back. With a triumphant bellow, the Bulgarian dived on top of him, clawing for his eyes.

Carter met the dive with a knee to the stomach, rolling

away and up on his feet before the other man could get a handhold.

Malenkov came to his feet with a snarl and rushed Carter again, hands outstretched, seeking a vulnerable spot. Carter slipped the rush, spun him with a hook to the ribs, then crossed with a smoking right to the bleeding face.

Malenkov staggered backward, hands at his sides and spitting teeth.

"Die, Malenkov," Carter hissed. "Lie down and die."

No charge this time, only a blind, staggering walk toward Carter.

The Killmaster measured and kicked hard just under the left kneecap. Malenkov went down on his right knee, clutching his left.

The eyes staring up at Carter were vacant now, but there was a message: acceptance. The eyes said it all: "Finish it."

Carter did. He stepped slightly to the side and raised his arm. The side of his right hand came down across Malenkov's neck like an executioner's sword.

The spine cracked, the head lolled to an odd angle, and the body fell forward into the mess on the floor.

Carter took a minute to get his breath. Then he went to the sink and washed the blood from his hands, arms, and face. He found a cotton towel hanging on a rusted nail over the workbench and used it to dry himself.

The two brothers were standing at the door. Gordo was grinning. Angel's face was impassive as he stared down at Malenkov's broken body.

"I don't think, señor," Angel said, "that you much liked this guy."

"Not much," Carter growled, walking past them to the big room where he divested himself of the rubber trousers and boots. "Give me about an hour, and then get rid of him," he said. "I assume you know places where he'll never be found."

Angel nodded. "It will be as if he was never born."

The Killmaster hit the door and gulped great lungfuls of fresh air as he moved to the car.

FOUR

Viktor Prokudin nodded to the guard and walked on through the side door of the embassy. He turned left out of the courtyard and moved toward the rear of the complex where the official cars were kept in a huge garage.

He was just approaching the wide double doors when the gate to his right, a hundred yards down the drive, opened and a long Mercedes pulled in.

It was Oleg Grechko's official car.

Prokudin stood, frozen in the glare of the powerful headlights. *Over,* he thought, *it's over.*

The car rocked to a halt, disgorging two men from the front and two from the rear. The fifth and last man out of the car was Oleg Grechko himself.

He headed directly for Prokudin, his wide, flat face expressionless, his cold blue eyes like glittering ice.

At sixty, Grechko would have been tall had he ever straightened up from a perpetual slouch. He carried his thin body like a wire question mark that somebody, at one time, had tried to straighten out but had given up on halfway through.

"Viktor, where is my wife?" he rasped to Prokudin. "Why did you not deliver her to the restaurant as you were instructed?"

Prokudin's agile mind was going a hundred miles an hour. He was close, so close. He was sure the references in the computer had given him the name. He couldn't give up now.

"I tried, Comrade Colonel, I swear, but . . ."

"But what?"

"She had been . . . drinking, much more than usual. I saw her to the car, then . . ."

"Speak, man! What happened?"

I am trying to speak, damn you! Give me a moment, I'm making this up as I go along!

"As I was going around to the driver's side, she locked the doors. She drove off, Comrade Colonel, before I could do anything."

The bent body bent more. Grechko staggered. He might have fallen had not his aide, Major Yegerov, jumped forward and clutched his arm.

"She's run, Yegerov," Grechko whispered. "Malenkov was right. The traitor was my own wife . . ."

Prokudin's insides turned to jelly. Could what he was hearing be the truth? Had the person they had been suspecting all along be, not himself, but Amalia?

"Oleg, what are you talking about? What is it?"

The *rezident*'s head came up, the usually clear blue eyes suddenly milky. "I was going to tell you later, Viktor, if it was true. For some time we have suspected a leak. We even thought it might be you. Hell, everyone was suspect, even me . . . even Yegerov here. Two days ago Malenkov arrived from Moscow. He was sure he had uncovered enough proof . . ."

"Amalia?" Prokudin said.

"Yes. She must have suspected that it was over when Malenkov arrived."

Yes, Prokudin thought, *I did.*

"Comrade Colonel . . ." Yegerov said, urgency in his voice.

"Yes, yes," Grechko said, nodding, "we must find her. Issue weapons. Use the cars, go in teams of two. Report back here on the car radios every half hour."

Yegerov was already moving into the garage to issue orders.

The *rezident* laid his hand on Prokudin's shoulder. "You drove her most of the time, Viktor. You knew her haunts, her habits. People, even drunken spies and traitors, stick to their habits. Ride with Ivan Yegerov, Viktor. Find Amalia and bring her back to me, so I can make her pay!"

Prokudin stole a glance at his watch. It was eleven o'clock sharp. *Damn, damn, damn!* he thought. *How will I ever get away from Yegerov in time?*

Tasseled corn bobbed in unfenced fields to either side of the road. Bean plants clutched and climbed eight-foot stakes in the moonlight. The heart of the city was ten miles behind him now, and he was dropping out of the shaggy mountains into a cup-shaped valley.

There were no street signs and no signs of human habitation except for a windowless shack now and then with chickens and maybe a goat foraging in the grassless enclosure around it.

The plans for the place of rendezvous had been made nearly two years earlier. To Carter's knowledge, they had never been updated. That was a mistake. Landmarks could change, a fire could remove one of the shacks, or a landslide could obscure a road completely. It was common in rural Mexico. Roads were rarely repaired when they were destroyed. A detour was devised and it became the new road.

He rounded a wide curve. Coming out of it was an incline. The nose of the Trans-Am lifted and, in the lights, he saw it.

A hundred yards farther on, the lights fell across a cockeyed wooden sign. It was weathered and the letters were scarcely legible, but enough remained for Carter to read CASA GUILLERMO, and in Spanish, NO TRESPASSING.

He swung off into the rutted lane and dropped the car into low gear as he climbed. Minutes later the lane widened and then opened onto what had once been the wide driveway in front of the hacienda.

It was a rambling, one-story building that had gone to ruin slowly and picturesquely. The stucco walls sported huge cracks and the wide front door hung open on one hinge. There was a pile of bricks in the front yard, as if someone were going to repair the ruined chimneys and had just given up. Most of the glass had been broken out of the windows. Those that were still intact were high up, and now they reflected the blue moonlight a smoky gray.

There was a large outbuilding to the left, its barn doors yawning wide, and beyond that a corral, the fence posts still standing but most of the rails down.

Carter drove on by the shell of the big house and into the barn. He cut the headlights and then the engine.

The silence was like a graveyard.

From the trunk he took the shotgun, the rifle, and the sack of grenades. He also filled his pockets with the spare clips and shells.

Logically, he wouldn't need all the hardware just to make the meet with Mayflower.

If the person coming was indeed Mayflower.

Carter wasn't taking any chances.

He carried the rifle and bag. He slung the shotgun over his shoulder, barrel down, and turned back toward the main house.

The heavy rear door was intact and unlocked. Carter stepped through into the wide, cool dimness of what had once been the kitchen. His feet echoed hollowly on the tile floor.

He paused.

No sound except the light breeze outside.

It didn't take long to find the trapdoor in the ceiling of one of the bedrooms. When he finally got it open, he climbed out onto the roof. He made a nest for himself against one of the ruined chimneys, lit a cigarette, and settled in to wait.

It was a combination cantina, grocery store, and garage. Produkin stepped through the screen door and let it bang behind him. He nodded his head as he approached the car. Ivan Yegerov sat impatiently behind the wheel.

"Da?"

"Two of the men at the bar said they saw her about a half hour ago," Prokudin lied.

"Good," Yegerov replied. "Which way?"

"There, north, heading into the mountains."

Dirt swirled beneath the rear wheels as the tall Russian floored the Mercedes. Then the tires screamed as they found the asphalt of the narrow, two-lane road.

Prokudin lit a cigarette, forcing his hands to remain steady. He squirmed in the seat to take the pressure off his ribs where the Stechkin automatic dug into him.

"Something?" Yegerov asked.

"No . . . the gun. I'm just not used to wearing it."

Beside him, Yegerov smiled and shoved down harder on the accelerator.

Prokudin concentrated on the tiny ribbon of black road stretching before them. He went over the route in his mind. In a few minutes they would cross an unused railroad track. Then they would pass the small village of Mayalpa.

About six miles beyond the village there was a turn, over-land on a rarely used road.

From there it was eighteen miles up to the hacienda.

Soon, Prokudin thought, *I will have to do it soon. There are no more gas stations or cantinas where I can go in, ask for change, and come back with the lie that someone inside has seen Amalia Grechko pass.*

Yegerov had the car up to seventy now. They flew through the tiny village and, in no time, Prokudin saw the road come up. He waited until they were just past before he called out.

"Stop . . ."

"What is it?" The tires screamed as Yegerov pulled the car into a slide.

"Back there, the road. I think I saw fresh tire marks turning off."

Yegerov idled back to the road. He crimped the wheel until the lights were shining up the track, slid the lever into "park," and got out of the car.

Slowly, Prokudin eased from the passenger seat. As he stood, he pulled the Stechkin from the holster and thumbed off the safety.

There is nothing else I can do, he thought. *I can't leave him free to find a telephone. I will have to kill him.*

"You are right, Viktor," Yegerov called out. "These are fresh tracks, and new tires with good, deep tread. No peasant around here would have new tires on his car or truck."

Yegerov stood up, his body a perfect target in the glare of the headlights. Prokudin brought the automatic up as he stepped from behind the door.

He must have missed the first time he fired. He heard Yegerov shout his name and then the man was running. Prokudin leveled the automatic, gripping his right hand with his left, and fired again, twice.

There was a shouted scream and Yegerov's body lifted into the air. He seemed to sail for a few feet, and then he disappeared into the flood runoff beside the road.

Prokudin didn't bother to check the kill. In fact he couldn't. In the fourteen years he had been in the KGB, he had never been called upon to kill. The truth was, he disliked killing altogether. Seeing all the covert killing his comrades did was one of the many reasons he had become a traitor.

And now, tonight, so that he could make good his defection, he had killed, twice.

But, sick as it made him feel, he could still move. He dived back into the Mercedes and quickly slid over into the driver's seat. He yanked the gear lever into "drive," and the powerful engine roared as he spun, fishtailing up the dirt road.

In seconds the taillights were only tiny points of red in the night. When they disappeared completely, Ivan Yegerov crawled up out of the ditch.

With one hand he brushed off his suit. With the other, he pulled the powerful radio from the holster under his own arm, where his Stechkin would normally be.

"Chase, this is Target. Target to Chase. Do you read?"

"This is Chase, Target. Read you loud and clear. What is your situation?"

"He bought it, all of it. He is off the highway heading northeast. Are you following?"

"The beeper is loud and clear, Target. Get out on the road. We should reach you in about ten minutes . . ."

The driver of the first chase car, Peter Milonovitch, hung the hand mike back on the dash and increased his speed. Out of the corner of his eye he saw Oleg Grechko's hawklike face break into a leering grin as he watched the tiny yellow dot progress on the portable radar scope in his lap.

"He will lead us directly to his contact."

"Pardon me, Comrade Colonel," Milonovitch said, "but wouldn't it have been less risky to take him right at the embassy?"

"Of course it would have," Grechko rasped. "But we must find out how much of Project High Dive our dear Comrade Prokudin has already passed on in the last day or two."

Milonovitch drove in silence for a few more miles.

"Why do you suppose he killed your wife?"

The narrow shoulders in the other seat shrugged. "Who knows? Perhaps he thought that he could shift our suspicions to her. The fool Malenkov thought the traitor was my wife. Perhaps in his stupidity he said something to Prokudin. Who knows?"

In the driver's seat, Peter Milonovitch suppressed the chill that raced up his spine.

He could still see Oleg Grechko's face in the moonlight when they had sat, hidden, a few hours earlier and watched Prokudin kill his wife.

Then, like now, Comrade Grechko's face was calm, emotionless, undisturbed.

FIVE

The Killmaster dug his penlight out of his pocket when he saw the car turn and begin to bounce up the rutted lane. Halfway up, the car halted. The lights went off for a full minute. Then they went on and off three times quickly.

When they went black the last time, Carter counted to twenty and flashed the penlight three times. The headlights came back on and the car slowly progressed forward toward the house. Carter grabbed his gear and literally dived into the bedroom below. By the time he was crouching by the front door, the Mercedes was just halting ten yards away.

The engine quieted and the headlights were killed. A tall figure slid from the driver's side, then froze at the sound of Carter's voice.

"Leave the lights on!"

"I am Mayflower," the figure replied.

"Bully for you. Leave the fucking lights on and get in front of the car!"

The Killmaster waited until the tall, extremely handsome man was dead center in the glare of the lights before he stepped through the door and moved to the car.

Cradling the shotgun under one arm, he shined the penlight inside the Mercedes. Satisfied there was no one there, he grabbed the keys from the ignition and checked the trunk. It, too, was devoid of lurking bodies.

45

Then, and only then, did he kill the lights and join the other man.

"Lift 'em!"

"What?"

"Your arms," Carter growled, nudging the man's belly with the barrel of the shotgun, "get 'em out like you're on the cross."

The arms went out and up. The Killmaster patted him down and lifted the Stechkin from the shoulder rig. Even before he smelled the barrel, Carter could tell from the weight that the automatic had been fired.

"You shoot somebody with this?"

The man nodded. "Why are you doing this? I am Mayflower."

"You damn well better be," Carter hissed. "Got a date?"

"April 20, 1889," came the reply. "Have you a name?"

"Schicklgruber," Carter said, and both men relaxed. The agreed connection had been made. April 20, 1889 was Adolf Hitler's birthday, and Schicklgruber was his father's name. Carter reached forward and slid the Stechkin back into the man's holster. "Okay, Mayflower, let's talk."

"My name is Viktor Prokudin. I am . . . was, first assistant to Colonel Oleg Grechko. My principal job was liaison to the code section and domestic cells where we were stationed."

Carter whistled. "Washington had you tagged as a code clerk. I'm surprised you survived so long as a mole with that high a rank."

Prokudin shrugged. "I had a secondary source of information and a strong ally, Grechko's wife, Amalia. I was her lover for several years."

Carter mulled this over for a few seconds, and then told Prokudin what he had learned from Gripon Malenkov.

The Russian only nodded. "That's why I am safe. They still think the mole is Amalia."

"They won't think that very long when they break her down," Carter growled. "I understand she's a drunk. She'll talk . . . fast."

"No." Prokudin paused as if he were trying to think of what to say. "She won't be able to tell them anything. I killed her earlier this evening."

"Is that who you shot?"

"No, I pushed her off a bridge in the embassy Volvo. She drowned."

Carter didn't even blink. "Good. And Malenkov won't be telling them anything either. For the same reason. Are you sure you weren't followed?"

Prokudin explained what had happened at the embassy and after.

"But you didn't check the body?" Carter said, little hairs prickling on the back of his neck.

"There was no point. I hit him twice . . . he fell into the ditch . . . I—"

Carter had held up his hand for silence.

"Hear it?"

"No."

"A car . . . maybe two. A long way off, maybe three, four miles. But up here, on a night like this, you can hear a snake go over a rock."

Suddenly Carter's hand flashed under the other man's coat and came out again with the Stechkin.

"This Yegerov . . . you killed him with this?"

"Yes . . . I fired three times. I missed with the first shot, but I am sure I hit him with the second and third bullets."

Carter was pulling the slide so fast his hand was a blur. As cartridges ejected and fell to the ground, he spoke.

"In case you're not up on it, the Stechkin is the premier

Soviet automatic pistol. A novice could hit a man-sized target easily at up to seventy-five yards . . ."

"I was no more than twenty feet. Yegerov is dead . . ."

Carter was waving the now-empty automatic in front of Prokudin's eyes, shutting him up.

"The Stechkin A.P.S., without shoulder stock but with a fully loaded clip, weighs one point seven pounds. You said you fired three rounds. When I hefted this piece before, the little man in the back of my brain was telling me by the weight of the gun that the clip was probably empty."

Prokudin was shaking his head. "I don't understand . . ."

Carter shined the penlight on the ground. The nine "live" shells in the middle of the beam were blanks.

It took Carter less than a minute and a half to find the beeper bug under the Mercedes's dash. He held it up so Prokudin could see it.

"I wish the whole KGB were like you," he hissed.

The man was shaking visibly now, and a lot of the color had drained from his face. "I am only a code expert and an analyist. I've never had complete training—"

"I can believe it." Then Carter remembered that for the last seven years this guy's ass had been on the hot seat. All that time he had lived in daily fear, and he hadn't cracked. "Hey . . . sorry. See, being a smart-ass, well, it's the American way. You can shoot, though?"

"Yes, yes, I can shoot." Then Prokudin added, "And I can hit something, with real bullets."

"Good enough." Carter handed him the shotgun, the rifle, and the keys to the Trans-Am. "My car's in the barn, there. Turn it around, but put it back out of sight. And don't use the lights."

Prokudin turned away, then paused and turned back. "Aren't you going to smash the bug?"

"Nope. I want 'em to follow it right on in."

The Russian was smart enough not to ask any more questions. He trotted toward the barn and Carter made a beeline for the house. He hit four windows before he found a set of drapery cords that weren't rotted away.

Booby-trapping the rear door was no problem. He kicked two holes in the plasterboard about six feet down the hall from the door. Then he tied two lengths of cord to the inside knob and ran them to the grenades. When the grenades were wedged firmly in the plasterboard, he attached the cords to the pins.

The front door was even simpler. He used a trip wire from sill to sill, and planted the grenades in the moldy dirt of a long-dead plant.

It took less than a minute to scrounge old rags and paper from the downstairs rooms. These he placed in a large wastepaper basket, and placed the basket on the floor in one of the center rooms.

He used his cigarette lighter on the paper. The paper would ignite the rags and they would burn much more slowly. From outside the house it would look like candle-light or a small fireplace fire. Carter hoped that the bad guys would assume he and Mayflower were conferring around the fire.

Carefully, he stepped over the trip wire at the front door and darted to the Mercedes. Two more grenades were set, one on each side of the front seat, with the trip cords attached to the door's armrests.

The last thing he did before cinching the driver's-side cord and shutting the door was slide the keys into the ignition.

Anybody looking in the window on either side of the car would see those keys, and want them so that Carter and Mayflower couldn't use the Mercedes for an escape.

Prokudin had turned the Trans-Am around and backed it deep into the barn. When Carter got there, he was sitting tensely behind the wheel. The Killmaster got in beside him.

"What's your first name?"

"Viktor."

"Okay, Viktor, here's the scoop. I'm going to be over in those rocks at the head of the lane." As he spoke, he checked the loads in the M-1 and the Savage, and arranged shells and spare clips in various pockets so he could get to them fast.

"Do you really think they set me up, that they followed me?"

"I do," Carter said, nodding. "It's just a question of how far they baited you. And don't kid yourself—they'll be here. Give me that Stechkin of yours."

Prokudin handed over the Russian automatic. Carter's Luger took 9mm shells. Methodically, he transferred shells from the Luger's clip to the Stechkin's, shoved the clip home, and handed it back to the Russian.

"You thought you heard two cars . . ."

"Right," Carter said, getting out of the car.

"That means there are probably eight of them. We won't have a chance."

Carter chuckled low in this throat. "Just wait and see, Viktor. How well can you drive?"

Prokudin shrugged. "As well as most, I'd say."

"All right. When you hear the first shot, the first boom, or a shout from me, *go!* And I mean go like hell."

"But what about you?"

"I'm getting to that. Swing to the right out of the barn. Then go hard left, straight through that fence, and hit the lane. Once you've committed, get down, and I mean *way* down, because there's bound to be at least one in the lane firing at you. Hopefully from the rocks I'll see them come out of cover for a shot at you."

For the first time since Prokudin had arrived, he smiled. "And you'll pick them off."

"As many as I can. When you hit the road, turn right. About a quarter of a mile up, there's a stand of trees. Park on the road, then get out of the car and into the trees. Wait for me there. And shoot anything around you that moves."

Prokudin was about to say something else, but the shadowy figure was already gone.

Carter kept in the shadows and moved in a wide arc around the open area in front and to the side of the house. In no time he was in the rocks and climbing.

Carefully, he chose a spot where he had uninterrupted vision for 360 degrees. Then he set up his hardware, balancing the M-1 and the Savage on the rocks and arranging the remaining three grenades on the ground by his side.

Carter could hear them but he couldn't see them. The crunch, barely audible, of a broken twig underfoot to the rear of the house. The slight scrape of something metallic against stone in the other pile of rocks beyond the barn. The low grunt of a man below and to Carter's right, near the mouth of the lane.

They seemed to be coming in from every direction. That meant Mayflower's guess had been right. Two carloads, probably eight men, maybe more.

Then Carter saw movement. There were two of them, flat against the stucco, coming around the corner of the house.

Carter brought up the M-1 and started searching with the scope. Then he got them, a Mutt-and-Jeff pair, both with slung machine pistols, powerful Stechkins like the one Prokudin had under his coat. Only these two were using shoulder stocks. That made the automatics deadly accurate at a distance.

No matter, Carter thought, thumbing off the safety on the M-1; these two would be the first to go when the fireworks started.

Then the little one, Jeff, dropped to his belly and began to crawl. He disappeared behind the Mercedes, and Carter smiled. He moved the cross hairs on the scope to Mutt, and waited.

The interior light of the Mercedes flicked on for only a second before the man put a finger over the button to kill it. Carter saw the head and shoulders raise up, the free arm reach out to retrieve the keys. . . .

And then all hell broke loose.

The interior of the big car disintegrated and Jeff went with it. Instantly, the upholstery caught and the Mercedes was an inferno lighting up the area.

Mutt was thrown back against the front wall of the house by the blast, but he was moving, bringing up the machine pistol and looking for something to hit.

Carter put two slugs from the M-1 into his chest and he dropped out of sight.

The Trans-Am engine was roaring and Mayflower was rolling. Carter tracked him out of the corner of his eye as he concentrated on the action to come.

One Russian had bolted across the open area on the far side of the house and taken a header through what was left of a window on that side. He was scarcely through when gunfire erupted inside.

The Trans-Am whirled by below Carter, got traction in the courtyard, and took off toward the mouth of the lane. One of the Russians appeared in its path and started spraying. Carter saw the windshield explode, but evidently

Mayflower was staying down. The car stayed under control and kept barreling ahead.

The Killmaster brought the M-1 around, but there was no need. Before he could get off a shot, the car had struck the kneeling man. There was a brief scream and the body was sailing out of sight in the trees.

Two more were running around Carter's end of the house. He flipped the M-1 to full auto and fired. One of the men literally came apart. The other disappeared behind the burning pyre of the Mercedes.

Suddenly there was another explosion and the rear of the house went up.

Carter had tried to count, but it was useless. Too much, too soon.

The one behind the Mercedes was firing at Carter now, on his feet backing away from the heat of the fire toward the house.

Carter jammed a new clip into the M-1 and fired just in front of him, forcing him toward the door. He turned and ran right into the trip wire.

Pieces of him were still coming down when Carter decided it was time to go. He slung the M-1, cradled the shotgun, and got to his feet. He pulled the pin on the remaining two grenades, threw them toward the woods at the head of the lane, and took off.

Prokudin hit the top of the lane with both hands fighting the wheel, his left foot on the brake, his right on the accelerator, pumping them both.

He knew he was cut from the flying glass of the windshield and the passenger-side window. He didn't know where he had gotten it, but he could feel blood running down his arms and face.

The Trans-Am was halfway down the lane when Prokudin saw Peter Milonovitch step from the trees right into the rocking headlights of the car.

"You fool!" Prokudin screamed.

The beams from the Trans-Am spotlighted him. His stance was cocky and self-assured as the machine pistol came up in both hands.

Prokudin wanted to shout at him, to warn him. But the cry stuck in his throat even as his foot jammed the accelerator.

The car was almost on Milonovitch before he realized that his comrade meant to kill him. Suddenly he couldn't decide which way to leap. Instead, he drew in his stomach and thrust back his hips, as if that were going to help.

The hood ornament impaled him in the chest. His face registered surprise as the car carried him the short distance to a tree. His cry was deep-throated panic and it died like a siren as he exhaled his breath. His last breath.

The car smashed him against the tree with a clattering roar. The impact nearly severed Milonovitch at the waist. His arms flew to the side like a man crucified. The flattening of his body added a strange squashing sound to the metallic clang of the shattering car. It was a sound that could have nauseated Prokudin if he had thought about it at all.

Prokudin reversed the Trans-Am just enough to get back into the lane, dropped the gear back into "drive," and roared on toward the road.

Carter came over the last heap of rocks right into a hornet's nest. But he had an advantage: he had heard the engine of their car, and their shouted arguments as to what to do next, before they heard him.

He had already unlimbered the shotgun, so that by the time he hit the rise both guns were firing.

There were three of them, two outside the car and one, the driver, trying to move it.

The first one tried to bring his Stechkin into play, but froze when he saw the man hurtling down at him from the rocks. Instead of the Stechkin in his right hand he threw his left up imploringly.

The first slug hit him in the armpit, came out his shoulder, and embedded itself in his neck. The impact flopped him over onto his belly and the second shot went in his back, skidding him half a foot farther. A third bullet severed his spinal column, leaving him to twitch and bounce on the ground like a squirming worm on a hook. He screamed, knowing he was going to die and anxious to get it over with.

Carter had a moment to gloat. Then his eyes shifted toward the car to see a Bulgarian Luger coming up as the second man spun from behind the rear of the car.

Carter let go with the M-1.

The first slug clipped off the top of the man's right ear. A second bullet blew away his middle, and a third put a hole through both his cheeks, taking teeth with it from both sides of his mouth. He fell to the ground, his hands trying to keep his insides from falling out.

As he fell, Carter saw a third man trying to struggle from the car. He held a small revolver and fired as he moved. The Killmaster felt a burning sensation at his right side and a tug at his left arm.

He dropped to his knees and poured both loads from the Savage toward the car. Glass shattered and pellets careened off steel. He heard a scream from inside the car and the door banged open.

The man who leaped out had an arm dangling by the tendons only. It flopped like a broken wing on a bird, but his good hand still held the pistol. A young stocky type, the pain disoriented him. His face had become a hideous Halloween mask, one eye hanging partway out of its socket, the tip of his nose gone and his upper lip torn away.

Carter fired the M-1 point-blank, and both halves of the body toppled back into the car.

The Killmaster paused only long enough to check the damage. He was creased on the right side. Not bad, but he was losing blood. A slug had passed clear through his left forearm.

Slinging the shotgun, he jammed a fresh clip into the M-1 and took off at a dead run for the road.

Seconds later he sensed rather than saw the asphalt beneath his feet. He turned right and kept running, holding his right arm against his side to stop the bleeding as much as possible.

Then he saw the car.

"Viktor . . . Viktor, it's me!"

The words had scarcely left his lips when Prokudin came bolting from the trees. "I'm here!"

"Let's get out of here!" Carter roared, climbing into the car. "You'll have to drive . . . they got me in the arm."

Prokudin dived into the driver's seat and the car roared to life. The tires screamed and in seconds the speedometer was hovering at seventy.

"Which way?"

"North," Carter replied, digging a map from the glove compartment. "And stay on the side roads."

Using a penlight, the Killmaster studied the map. He was having trouble making his eyes focus.

Shit, he thought, *that's all we need now, for me to pass out!*

SIX

False dawn was breaking over the mountains when Carter directed Prokudin to pull over to the side. They were atop a rise; below them was a decent-sized village.

"That's Milongo," Carter said, tapping the map on his lap. "We'll have to dump this bucket of bolts here and get another car."

Beside him, Prokudin sighed. "Why don't we just turn ourselves in to the *federales* and demand that they take us to an American embassy?"

Carter painfully shook his head. "Viktor, old chap, how many party cells have your people got in Mexico?"

"A hundred and fifty, more in the north."

"Grechko and his troops have probably got the word out to every one of them. They are already tracking us by now. We turn ourselves in, we die in some grubby little jail before anyone from Mexico City can get to us."

"Then what are we to do? It is too far to the U.S. border."

"I know," Carter said, sitting up and grimacing with the effort. "That's why we're not going to the border. We never were."

Prokudin's eyebrows shot up. "What?"

"We're getting new wheels and heading south. That was the plan all the time. My people are waiting for us in a villa near Veracruz. You'll be debriefed there, and then taken to the Caribbean." Carter pushed the map to the floor and checked his wounds. He was still bleeding heavily.

"How is it?" Prokudin asked.

"Not good."

"This village is probably large enough to have a doctor."

"How's your Spanish?" Carter asked.

"Excellent."

"Okay, let's go. Doc first, car second."

At the bottom of the hill there was an intersection. A tiny, overgrown cemetery was on one corner, a green-shuttered old house with cracked pink plaster walls on the third. The fourth corner was taken up by a modern gas station and repair garage.

In front of the garage, an attendant in faded overalls and hip boots washed an old Cadillac.

"Ask him where you can find a doctor," Carter said. "Tell him your friend was bitten by a dog in the hills last night."

Prokudin was back in less than a minute. "He says there's a doctor four doors this way from the church, sign out in front. He also wants to know if we want our car repaired."

Carter had been eyeing the old Cadillac. It had the usual battered look, the original paint job was almost gone, and there were potted geraniums wired to both sides of the windshield. But the tires looked new, and ten-to-one it was in better running condition than the now battered Trans-Am.

"Ask him how he'll trade."

"For that?" Prokudin cried.

"For that," Carter said, and grinned.

Prokudin moved back to the man, haggled for a few minutes, and returned. "He says, 'even up,' your car is a mess."

"Tell him to throw in two shirts and coveralls like his, a tank of gas, and a crate of those chickens out back, and he's got a deal."

Shaking his head, Prokudin relayed the message and returned. "It will be loaded and gassed up when we finish with the doctor."

They drove on into the village. Prokudin parked in front of a modest house. They waited until a vendor had moved his vegetable cart on down the street, and then, shielded by the Russian, Carter got out and staggered up the walk.

When the doctor answered the door in his pajamas, he was in a bad mood but agreed to treat Carter.

Between the two men they got him up on an examination table and the doctor cut away Carter's shirt. Then both wounds were carefully cleansed.

"Nasty," the doctor said, training a powerful light on Carter's side.

"Dog," the Killmaster murmured, "a very big dog."

The doctor eyed him sharply. "A dog did this?"

Carter smoothed two American hundreds out on the table. "Nasty dog. Came out of nowhere while I was taking a leak beside the road."

"What kind of dog?" the doctor asked, swabbing with alcohol.

Carter winced. "A chihuahua."

"Nasty bites for a chihuahua." He readied a needle for the stitches. "Have you had a tetanus shot?"

"No."

"Should have one. And this should be reported to the health authorities. A chihuahua, you say?"

"Yeah. And I don't need a shot, and the health authorities are too busy for such minor matters." Carter added two more hundreds to the pile.

The doctor nodded and started sewing. "We have some

very big, vicious chihuahuas in Mexico. But they are all healthy and rabies-free."

They were lucky. The Cadillac actually ran and ran well. Prokudin bought coarse bread, sausage, cheese, and a six-pack of beer, and they drove north out of the village.

About twenty miles on, they cut east toward the ocean.

"We'll hit a fair four-lane about ten miles up. But find a place to stop before then."

"Sleep . . . I hope?" Prokudin asked.

Carter nodded. "At the four-lane, we'll head back south after dark. With any luck they will be checking all the roads heading north, toward the border. By the time they catch on, we'll be in Veracruz."

Prokudin found a place high in the hills where it was cooler. He parked in the shade of a grove of trees. They wolfed down their makeshift picnic lunch and then climbed back into the car.

Carter lay in the back, sighed, and closed his eyes. He fell asleep almost immediately.

The sun was below the side of the car and dropping fast when his eyes popped open again.

Prokudin was in the front seat, fast asleep, his arms curled around the steering wheel. Carefully, so as not to wake the man, Carter got out.

The wounds were still painful, but as he limbered his body he realized that they would heal quickly.

He stretched, yawned, and walked through the sparse trees. The air was already becoming cool with the coming evening. It was fresh with the smell of plants and animals. Off to his right, a small herd of sheep grazed on the grass below the trees.

He was about to light a cigarette, when he heard it: a drone. Slowly it got louder, and then he saw it: a helicopter, small, a two-seater. It was coming over the hills straight for him.

He faded back into the trees and dropped into a crouch. The chopper passed close enough so he could see the pilot's features.

He watched it dive over a ridge to where the highway would be, and turn north. He turned and saw Prokudin about ten feet away, deeper in the trees. "You see it?"

"I saw it," Prokudin replied grimly, "only too well. The passenger in the right-hand seat was Oleg Grechko."

"Shit," Carter hissed, and went back to the car. He yanked out the map and spread it over the hood. "We'll have to get another car as soon as it's dark."

"Where?" Prokudin asked.

"Here, in Tampico. Only this time we'll steal one."

"The gas station attendant?"

Carter shrugged. "Or the doctor, or any one of the dozen or so people who saw us on the street."

Prokudin sighed. "I know it's a vast and well-put-together organization. I put it together."

The taxi traveled the open expanse of Saint Peter's Square, headed along the bank of the Tiber, then turned east toward Trastevere. The area was ancient, one of the most densely populated sections of Rome. The streets twisted and turned in every direction.

"Stop here."

The driver pulled to the curb, and accepted his fare and a generous tip. He also got a generous view of a well-rounded thigh as the woman stepped from the cab. She slammed the door and walked back in the direction they had just traversed.

The driver shook his head. This area was no place for a

woman at night, especially a beautiful woman. He hoped she knew what she was doing.

Number 12 was a drab, two-story brick house in a little-used cul-de-sac off Via della Lungara. Its brickwork was impregnated with decades of grime, the painted stucco tired and peeling.

The woman walked along the pavement to the gate of the house, went up the steps, and rapped lightly with a gloved hand. She heard the click of the shield over the peephole on the other side and then the bolt sliding. She slipped through and the door was closed behind her by a short, bald man with a foul-smelling cigarette dangling from the corner of his mouth.

"He's waiting in the study. This way." The man spoke English with a heavy Slavic accent.

The woman followed him up a short staircase and down a wood-paneled hallway. There was, about the whole house, a musty, unused smell.

The door to the study was open. The short, bald man nodded her in and closed the door silently behind her.

It was a small, austerely furnished room made dim by the closed drapes and the dark leather volumes lining the walls.

At the far end of the room a man in baggy trousers and a slightly soiled white shirt with no tie warmed his hands at a gas fire. He was a big man. What had once been the body of a superbly conditioned athlete had given way to the paunchiness of middle age. His once swelling chest had slipped to crowd the area over his belt. His waist had been level at one time, but now it was elevated by nearly thirty degrees as his stomach pushed the front of his belt downward.

This, she thought, watching him waddle toward her as

she peeled off her gloves, *is the man I must depend on for the success of my mission?*

"How was your flight?" he said, extending his hand. His English, like the other man's, was also heavily accented.

"Like all flights, boring," she replied, managing not to wince as she felt the clamminess of his palm. "What is the latest?"

"The same," he answered with a shrug, "as of a few hours ago. They are still looking for Prokudin, but the last report was that he had not crossed into the United States."

"Grechko is a fool," she snapped, slapping her gloves against her leg. "The moment he discovered who the traitor was, Prokudin should have been eliminated."

"True, but interrogation of both Prokudin and his American contact would have told us how much of the project has been relayed."

She paced, firing her words over her shoulder. "And now, if they are not caught and terminated, the whole of High Dive is lost. Three years of work, gone!"

"There is a consolation."

"Oh?"

He nodded. "The progress file on High Dive was altered in the computer. Another name was substituted for yours under your code name."

"Is that supposed to make me feel easier about making the cruise? How can we know that Prokudin didn't get into the master file before the name was changed?"

Nervously, the man popped two antacid tablets into his mouth. His ulcer was acting up and this woman wasn't helping it. He was getting too old for field work, especially as control of a project with the magnitude of High Dive.

"We can't, of course, be sure, but we feel the percentages are on our side."

She whirled, stomping her foot. "Percentages? Don't talk to me about percentages! I have to survive on that ship for twenty days. If Prokudin and his contact aren't found, if they manage to escape, you know someone will be sent to make sure I don't survive those twenty days!"

The man plucked a cigarette from his pocket. It was halfway to his lips when he saw her nose wrinkle. He discarded it.

"We are taking precautions. Two of our best first-division teams will be on the ship." From the desk behind him he lifted three eight-by-ten photographs and passed them to the woman. "The names they will be traveling under, and all the information about them you should know, is on the back of the photographs,"

She flipped the pictures over and quickly read down the résumés. It took her only a few seconds to digest the material. Then she lifted her head and, with her eyes closed, seemed to be mumbling to herself. Finished, she passed them back.

He accepted them and shook his head. "It is amazing how you do that."

"It's one of the reasons I was chosen for this job. With my memory, I never have to write anything down."

"Nothing?"

"Nothing, not a single figure or equation."

"Amazing."

"All right, I will have to accept what is. Now, what arrangements have been made to get me off the ship?"

Again he turned to the desk. This time he spread a large map across it and picked up a pencil to use as a pointer.

"Here is the complete route of the *Grecian Mist*. There will be three stops in ports under Soviet control . . . Varna, in Bulgaria, on the eleventh day of the cruise, Odessa, on day twelve, and Sevastopol, on day sixteen. Prior to entering the Black Sea, during the stop at Istanbul, you must make contact and choose which port and which day you wish to make your departure." He looked up, smiling. "So you see there will be no need to remain on the ship for the full twenty days of the cruise."

She wasn't smiling. "And how is it to be accomplished so that the others don't suspect that I have defected with their precious knowledge?"

"Aside from the fact that they will never dream that you could hold such a vast amount of information in your head, you will meet with an accident."

"And die?"

He nodded. "The ship's doctor is being taken care of right now in Miami. You will be pronounced dead, and, of course, the body will be removed in a friendly port."

"Very good." At last a small smile appeared on her lips. "Now let us go over the codes and contacts."

They talked for another half hour, the woman writing nothing of the intricate plan down. It all went into her head and stayed there. At the end of that time, she was ushered back to the front door by the bald-headed man.

"Luck," he said at the door.

"Intelligence," she barked back. "Luck is for the Western idealists."

He watched through a crack in the door until he could no longer hear her heels tapping on the sidewalk.

SEVEN

The lagoon was only about a mile inland from the brightly lit yacht basin and just south of the town's outskirts. But it was dark and desolate. Only one small lane led down to it from the larger road, and the trees and wild shrubbery around its perimeter were more than enough to block movement from any curious eyes.

They had found it after brazenly driving around Tampico for nearly an hour. Then they had scoured the area on foot until they found exactly what they wanted.

Beside the yacht basin was an enclosed parking lot. Inside were over forty vehicles, most of them belonging to the owners or crews of the yachts. From outside the fence, Carter had selected the dustiest of the machines, a late-model Jeep. It was a good bet that the owner of the Jeep was at sea and had been for quite a few days.

"That's the one we'll take," he said. "Now, you drop me off at the lagoon and take the Cadillac into Tampico. Trade it for anything that will run, and make sure the dealer gets a good look at your face."

By now, Prokudin didn't question Carter's judgment. He did exactly as he was told, rattling off in the old Cadillac in the direction of town. That had been over two hours ago, and now Carter was worried.

As brilliant as the Russian agent was, he wasn't a trained fieldman. Would he blow a simple thing like buying a car? Or were Grechko and his crew moving faster than

Carter guessed, and already waiting for them in Tampico? Or was the Russian still foolish enough to think he could waltz into a police station, ask for protection, and get it?

He popped another of the painkillers that the Mexican doctor had given him, and moved down to the edge of the lagoon. It was hot and humid. It probably hadn't cooled off more than five degrees since the sun had gone down. Sweat started on his face and trickled off his chin as he heard—or thought he could hear—the laboring motor of a car.

He listened intently.

There was no doubt about it. There was a car coming down the lane, grinding along in low gear. He could only hope it was Prokudin and not some local fisherman who had decided to do some night netting in the lagoon.

Carter slung the M-1 and, cradling the Savage, pushed his way back into the shrubs and knelt, eyeing the mouth of the lane. After several agonizing moments, the hood of a battered Chevy appeared, its engine laboring as the rear wheels spun on the loose sand.

Carter lifted the Savage, and then spotted Prokudin's face through the windshield in a shaft of moonlight. The Russian drove the Chevy directly to the edge of the lagoon and stopped.

Carter emerged from the shrubs and approached the car. "How did it go?"

"All right, I think," the other man announced through a broad grin. "I haggled and put as much accent in my Spanish as I could. At least three of them got a good make on me. And, just as you said, I parked the Cadillac right in front of the garage before I broke the key off 'by accident' in the ignition. They will be sure to see it and interrogate the men in the garage."

"Good man. How much?"

"Two hundred American and the Cadillac."

"You got robbed," Carter said with a laugh.

"I know," Prokudin sighed, hauling two paper bags from the front seat of the car. He looked more beat—and beat up—than Carter. There were deep shadows under his eyes and his face was lined with strain. "Hungry?"

"Starved," Carter replied.

They sat beside the car and Prokudin started emptying one of the bags. He handed the Killmaster a thermos bottle.

"Here is hot coffee. I got sandwiches and two plates of shrimp."

Carter poured coffee into the cap of the thermos as Prokudin emptied another small sack. "What's that?"

"Whiskey. You want a shot?"

"No. Not right now," Carter said. He gulped the sandwich in four bites and started in on a plate of shrimp. Prokudin didn't eat. He was fiddling with a small tape recorder. "Where did you get that?"

"In Tampico. I figured I'd better get this all on tape, just in case."

"Just in case what?" the Killmaster asked.

"In case," the Russian replied, not looking up, "I don't make it."

Carter ate the rest of the meal in silence. Viktor Prokudin wasn't a trained operative, but he had to hand it to the guy; the Russian was a realist and he had guts.

When he was finished, he tossed the garbage in the car and put the shift in neutral.

"Give me a hand."

Together they pushed the old Chevy into the lagoon and watched it sink out of sight.

"Okay," Carter said, "now they are looking for us in a beat-up old Chevy. Let's go steal us a Jeep!"

They approached the parking lot from the water side, along an inlet about two hundred yards deep. Other than natural sounds, it was quiet. A fish jumped out of the water about twenty feet away. Nearer the shore, a spoonbill grabbed a fish and swallowed it with a jerking motion of its slim head. Farther down the shore, the shallows were alive with feeding birds.

When they reached the fence, they both dropped to their knees. Prokudin went to work with the wire cutters while Carter at his back kept watch.

"Done."

They both went through, and Carter passed the M-1 and the Savage to Prokudin. Carter motioned him toward the Jeep and he took off for the gate. The ancient key padlock took only seconds to pick and he was back at the Jeep. It took less than a minute to hot-wire and start the Jeep.

"You drive, no lights. I'll get the gate. Don't rev the engine like that. Just nice and easy."

The Jeep was through the gate and Carter was just re-locking the padlock, when he sensed their presence.

The first one came up out of the hedge abutting the fence. He came at Carter as if to tackle him. Another was hurtling toward him from the other side.

It wasn't hard to figure. They had spotted Prokudin in Tampico and followed him. The purchase of the Chevy had pushed their luck just a little too far. After following them to the parking lot after leaving the lagoon, they had simply waited until both Carter and Prokudin were in an open space.

Carter butted the first one in the gut with his head. He

sailed into the back of the Jeep, but came again. The second one clubbed at Carter's head with the gun. The Killmaster sidestepped the blow and smashed his fist into the man's nose. He fell away, clawing at his bloody face.

The first one was back. He threw a body block into Carter's side that sent needles from the previous wound to the base of his brain.

Half blind with pain, Carter drove his fist into the man's gut.

There were four more of them coming down the road toward the Jeep on foot. Unlike the first two, these four had given up on taking live prisoners. They all had handguns and they were blasting away as they ran.

Prokudin flipped the Jeep's lights on, catching the four of them in the beams, and rolled out the door.

"Carter!"

The Killmaster caught the M-1, spun it in his hands, and sprayed. He got two on the first burst. Prokudin got another with a burst from the Savage.

The fourth one dived over the hood of the Jeep, firing point-blank at Prokudin as he sailed. The Russian seemed to dance out of the way. Carter slammed the butt of the M-1 into the shooter's head, spun the rifle, and put a stitching burst across his back before he hit the ground.

By the time Carter got around to the passenger side, Prokudin was already in and racing the engine.

"All right?"

"Right . . . go!" Carter shouted. "There are bound to be one or two more around here somewhere!"

The forward surge of the car snapped Carter back against the seat. His door swung open, then slammed shut with a metallic bang. Prokudin took the next corner on two wheels without lifting his foot from the accelerator. The tires screamed and the Jeep slewed around the corner.

"There!" the Russian shouted.

"I see 'em," Carter growled.

It was an old pickup, facing them. The driver was obviously trying to get it started as the Jeep hurtled toward them.

Carter jammed his last clip into the M-1 and got his knees up in the seat. Fifty feet from the pickup, he leaned out the window and sprayed.

He aimed for the radiator, then the windshield, and got both. As they sailed by, he could see from the bloody interior of the pickup's cab that they would have no pursuit from that quarter.

"Take a left and go like hell when you hit the highway," Carter said, slumping back into the seat.

"You think there will be more ahead?"

"No," Carter said, "not for a while at least. These weren't front-line troops. They were local boys, all of them. They probably got the word and our descriptions from Mexico City, and instead of passing it on, tried to be heroes themselves. Pull over there and stop at that phone booth."

He was out of the car while it was still sliding and into the booth. He didn't bother with change and dialed the operator direct.

"Operator, this is an emergency collect call. My name is Dr. Nicholas."

He gave the woman the number and heard it ring. The soft voice of David Hawk's right-hand gal, Ginger Bateman, accepted the charges.

"Go ahead, Doctor," the operator said, and clicked off.

"Nick?"

"Yeah. I got him out, but they've got our number. They've already tried for us twice."

"Where are you?"

"Just south of Tampico about three hours out. I'm going to have to stick to the speed laws part of the way. I don't want the *federales* in on it after all this . . ."

"Right. What's the vehicle?"

"A mud-brown Jeep, one headlight out. Mexican license plate Joe-Easy-X-ray-One-One-Five."

"Got it."

"I'll come in on the main highway and take the bypass at Veracruz. Give me a lead car and a chase car at the cutoff."

"Will do. You'll know the cars. Happy trails."

"Let's hope so. *Ciao*."

He hotfooted it back to the Jeep, only to find Prokudin stretched out in the rear. "I am afraid you will have to drive the rest of the way, my friend."

Carter cracked the door. The dome light went on and he leaned in. Even before Carter pried the man's sticky hands away from his belly, the Killmaster could see that he had caught one.

"Jesus . . ."

"Try not to hit too many bumps."

It was still dark, but gray was tingeing the horizon when they came down out of the hills toward Veracruz. The city spread across the face of the cliffs overlooking the ocean.

Carter had stopped twice to change the makeshift bandage around Prokudin's middle. For the last hour the Russian had been mumbling into the tape recorder. In answer to each of Carter's queries about his condition, the Killmaster had only gotten a grunt in reply.

"Veracruz, Viktor. Only a few minutes now."

A grunt in reply.

Carter hit the cutoff to the bypass flying, and saw two

late-model Fords fall in behind him. The first one hit his lights twice and came around alongside. The passenger, a hard-eyed black man with a thick mustache, saluted Carter and pointed up the road.

Carter hit the Jeep's light and tromped the accelerator. The other Ford fell back, covering the tail.

Abreast of the city, the left the main road and turned inland. About a mile on, the lead Ford left the two-lane asphalt and traveled up a twisting dirt track. It was still too dark to see the countryside clearly, but they seemed to be passing through an orchard or fruit grove of some kind. After several minutes, they rounded a bend and flew through high, open gates connected to an even higher stone wall.

Ahead, Carter spotted the house. It was nestled into the foothills, a tall, imposing stone building, showing the Spanish influence in its arches and masonry. It was brightly lit. In front was a circular drive, a pleasant sloping lawn, and a large fountain with splashing water.

Carter stopped behind the Ford and turned in the seat. "This is it, Viktor, we made it . . ."

The Killmaster didn't have to feel the man's pulse. He knew Prokudin was dead.

In the Russian's right hand was a carefully folded slip of paper. In his bloody left hand was the small tape recorder.

EIGHT

The Morris House was a discreet and very elegant all-suite hotel that catered to those who demanded privacy. A crimson-coated doorman bowed Dr. Everett Ellis out of the cab.

"Good evening, sir."

Ellis nodded and pressed a five in the doorman's hand. He enjoyed the man's surprised smile.

The good doctor liked to tip big. He could more than afford it, and it helped to relieve some of the natural inferiority he constantly felt.

Dr. Everett Ellis was immaculately dressed in a double-breasted black suit, a white shirt, and a gray tie. The suit had been tailored for him in London. It had cost him a thousand pounds, and fooled only Ellis himself about the body it covered.

Dr. Everett Ellis was far from the bon vivant he wanted to be. He was completely bald, very tall, and very fat. In spite of his weight, he moved gracefully on small, dainty feet in small, dainty shoes. He seemed to float through the hotel's revolving doors like a blimp heavy at the bottom.

The clerk, a tall, dark man with a jutting jaw and dark curly hair, looked up. "Yes, sir?"

"Miss Bonstedt, please. She is expecting me."

The clerk cocked an eyebrow but reached for the desk phone. He had registered the Bonstedt woman when she'd arrived. This one didn't fit with her.

"Your guest is here, madam . . . of course." He nodded, replaced the receiver, and smiled at Ellis, his face a blank.

Impossible, he thought. The man's head was round, his forehead low. His face was a healthy, rosy color, his tiny watery eyes were embedded in cushions of fat. A pale blond mustache grew over his little old-womanish mouth.

"You may go right up, sir. Suite eleven-oh-two."

Ellis walked toward the elevators. The clerk looked with amazement at the ten-dollar bill on the desk, and chuckled.

At Suite 1102, Lenore Bonstedt opened the door for the doctor. She smiled, extending her hand. "I am so glad you came, Everett."

God, he thought, kissing the back of her hand and stepping into the foyer, *I wouldn't miss it for half the money in my Swiss accounts!*

"I could hardly believe it when I got your message off my service."

But he had been hoping. Every day of the last cruise she had seemed to be around, looking at him with those smoldering green eyes. Even when he had gone ashore he ran into her. But he hadn't gotten up the nerve to visit her stateroom until the last night.

"Not tonight, darling," she had said. "In Miami. I will call you."

Just the way she had said it meant worlds.

And then the message on his service: "Dear Everett, I am at the Morris House. Come this evening. We'll have a quiet dinner, just the two of us, in my suite."

Now she ran her fingers over his cheek and he felt the shock as her flesh met his. She withdrew her fingers gently and led the way to a living room.

"A drink, Everett?"

"Just Perrier, please . . . my stomach."

"Of course."

The smile was cool and the eyes unreadable. She wore a floor-length, figure-fitting gown of deep blue, a cloth that winked in the somber light of the room and accented her blond hair. A heavy gold chain hung about her neck, disappearing in the cleavage of the low-cut bodice.

The suite was tastefully decorated, a perfect setting for her brooding beauty. The living area hinted at the East, lush draperies and a large tapestry, imitation Byzantine. There were curiously shaped lamps and a fine Oriental on the floor. The coffee table was marble, the couches thick with pillows of gold, yellow, and blue.

Ellis figured the suite went for about two grand a week. Good. That meant she had money as well as class and beauty. These were the three prerequisites Dr. Everett Ellis dreamed he would one day find in a woman.

He sat beside her on a couch, watching her light a cigarette with trembling fingers. He said, "You look terribly serious."

"I suppose I do." She glanced at him and pressed her lips together. "I—I've had news from my uncle that upsets me."

"I hope he's in good health."

"Oh, yes." She nodded quickly. "But there has been more trouble."

He leaned back, taking a case from his pocket and extracting a cigarette. He molded it before placing it between his thin lips.

"Of course I have given a lot of thought to your request, Lenore, but I just don't think it can be done."

"But, Everett, you said you can request and hire any assistant you want. And I assure you my uncle is a licensed medical doctor. He just has to get out of the country, that's all."

"I would love to help you, my dear, but I just cannot

afford to take such a risk," he replied. "How would I explain his jumping ship in some foreign port?"

She moved closer to him on the couch until her breasts were pressing against his pulpy bicep.

"Everett, you are our last resort . . ."

Sweat beaded his brow as his eyes bore into the deep valley between her swelling breasts. "Lenore," he choked, "I would do anything for you . . ."

"Then do this, Everett. Believe me, you will never regret it."

She took his hand and pressed it to one of her bulging breasts. His shirt was immediately soaked with perspiration.

"I can't. Anything else, but not this. There are many reasons I can't tell you about . . ."

Suddenly she was standing before him. "I will ask you one last time."

The perspiration turned cold on his body. Before him was another woman. Now her eyes were cold and hard, and he didn't like the tone in her voice.

"I cannot," he murmured.

"Is that your last word, Doctor?"

"It has to be."

"Excuse me."

She exited to the bedroom. Ellis mopped his face with a scented handkerchief. When she returned, it was with a short fur wrap over her shoulders.

Ellis stood. "Are we going out?"

"I am."

She moved into the foyer. Ellis followed. The door opened and she darted into the hall. Ellis tried to follow, but his way was suddenly blocked.

The man was inches taller than Ellis, with a flat face,

dull black eyes, and a thick neck. Beneath the beefy jacket were broad, beefy shoulders and a barrel chest.

"Who the hell are you?" the doctor blustered. "What is—"

From nowhere a rock-hard fist smashed into Ellis's face. He staggered back into the living room, crashed over the coffee table, and came down, hard, on his well-padded butt.

He sat, looking bewildered and hurt. He hadn't had time yet for any fear to set in.

The fear would come.

Ellis raised a quivering hand to wipe the dampness from his broken mouth. He brought a hand down, palm up, and stared at the sticky redness in disbelief.

His lips puckered and he tried not to cry.

The dark-haired giant heeled the door shut, locked it, and hooked the night chain in place.

"Why? You . . . you hit me," Ellis said as the man stepped over his legs and walked to the window.

There was no reply.

He drew the thick drapes over the huge picture window, blocking out the city lights and making the dim room even dimmer. When he had a lamp turned on, he lifted Ellis easily and pushed him back into the couch.

"Who the hell are you?" Ellis cried.

"My name, Doctor, is not important. And you can forget the woman. Her name is also unimportant, and it is not Lenore Bonstedt. But we know you . . . quite well."

"I don't understand."

"You will, fat man. You are Everett Addison Ellis. You graduated from the St. John's School of Medicine in 1967. Very low in your class, I might add. You financed your education by selling marijuana and small amounts of cocaine to your fellow students . . ."

"Oh, my God."

"You did your internship at Blessing General Hospital in Macon, Georgia. This period of your career was also undistinguished. While there, you sold amphetamines and barbiturates to street people to keep up your life-style . . ."

"Are you a cop?"

The man ignored him. "You went into private practice, but it bored you. Also, it wasn't very lucrative. You continued to deal in small quantities of dope. Three years ago, you took a cruise, and you were approached in Istanbul by a man who opened up a whole new world of riches for you."

Everett Ellis was shaking like a leaf now. He felt like the man dying and his life flashing before him. He put gentle fingers to his split lip and spoke around them. "What do you want? Money?"

The man unbuttoned his jacket. The wooden butt of a large automatic protruded above his belt. "See it?"

Ellis went pale. His fingers shook at his mouth and he shut his eyes.

The man slapped his face, then gripped his ears, hard. *"See it?"*

"Yes, yes, I see it."

"You might scream before I am finished, fat man, but scream softly. Don't make me kill you."

"W-why are you doing this?"

"You were given a chance to help us. You were even offered the woman's body in return."

Ellis's eyes went wide. "You're trying to trick me. I won't say anything until I've talked to my attorney!"

"Shit," the man hissed in disgust. "I am not police. I am not a narcotics investigator."

"Then who are you?"

"I am a convincer. I convince people, such as yourself, to do things that are in their own best interests."

"Like what?"

"There is a doctor here in Miami. He is already registered with the Nomad Lines. When the *Grecian Mist* sails the day after tomorrow, he will sail with it, as your assistant."

"I can't do that! I have an assistant—"

"Listen, fat man, I introduced myself to you with a punch in the mouth, and that's *all* it was, an introduction. I'll beat you until your own family wouldn't recognize the mess that's left. I'll rupture your kidneys and crush your larynx and maybe gouge out an eye, and sooner or later, you'll do anything I want you to do. But it will come too late to save your kidneys, your throat, your eyes."

Ellis's eyes were now bulging. "You wouldn't dare . . ."

The man heeled Ellis high on the left cheekbone, a short, powerhouse blow that delivered a maximum of jolt without much chance of a knockout. Ellis's head snapped back into the couch, bounced forward again. While his eyes were still clouded with shock, the man fisted him high in the right chest under and behind the nipple, a punishing, painful shot.

It took time for Ellis to recover. His nose had started to bleed and he made heavy gasping noises; he didn't wipe away the blood as he had before. It leaked down onto his shirt, blotting the material to the skin in ugly designs.

The man never blinked. "I can snap each of your fingers and break out your teeth."

"No, no," Ellis whined, "I'll do whatever you ask! Just don't hit me again!"

Suddenly the man actually smiled. "Good, that's good, fat man. Just sit still there and I'll get you a drink."

Ellis watched as the man brought a bottle and glass from the minibar. He brought a towel as well. Ellis rattled the bottle neck against the glass and took a big swallow before dabbing the towel at his face.

"Feel better, fat man?"

Ellis didn't reply.

"In this envelope is everything you need to know about your new assistant. I want you to contact the line, the ship, and him, right away. There isn't much time. Do you understand?"

Ellis nodded.

The man dropped the envelope in Ellis's lap. Then he took another, larger envelope from his inside jacket pocket. From this envelope he took several eight-by-ten glossy pictures and spread them out on the coffee table.

Ellis gagged when he saw them. It was all there, clear and sharp, in black and white.

They were pictures of him making the heroin pickup in Marseilles. Pictures of him with the two whores they always supplied him with when he picked up. More shots of him in the hotel room, putting the kilos of heroin in the false bottom of his medical bag. There were even pictures of him back here in Miami making the drop and getting paid for it.

"Just in case, fat man, you decide at the last minute not to help us."

They had it, all of it.

The big man's smile was thin and mean. "No choice, Doctor. You have no choice."

"No choice," Ellis echoed.

"If you don't cooperate, you'll have your choice of executioners . . . the heroin smugglers you mule for, or the drug enforcement people."

The man moved to the foyer.

"Clean yourself up before you leave, fat man. We wouldn't want anyone to think you had an accident."

Everett Ellis began to cry. Slowly and silently, and with his face working like a baby's, he began to cry.

NINE

The knock awakened Carter instantly. And just as quickly, he fought it and tried to force himself back to sleep.

It came again and he rolled to his side, pulling a pillow over his head. The moment his weight hit the wound, he yelped, came fully awake, and sat up.

At the same time, the door opened and a vision came in bearing a tray. Carter rubbed his eyes and the vision became Ginger Bateman.

"Good, you're up . . . partially."

"What time is it?"

"Eight . . . P.M.," she replied. "You've been out fourteen hours. I brought breakfast."

Carter watched her advance with the tray. A lot of her character came through her movement . . . head high, shoulders back, just enough sensual sway to her hips. She reeked of confidence, and Ginger Bateman had every reason to be confident.

Positionwise, she was the right hand of David Hawk, head of supersecret AXE.

Womanwise, she was beautiful, with thick auburn hair, sultry eyes, and a hundred twenty-five pounds of knockout figure on a five-foot-nine frame.

She set the tray across Carter's legs and tapped the bandage on his side. "How does it feel?"

"Like hell."

"And the arm?"

"Worse."

"You're right in form."

She lifted a napkin from one of the dishes on the tray. Beneath it were two miniatures of Chivas Regal.

It broke the ice, forcing a laugh from Carter. "God, you're a good nurse."

"Not really—I just know you."

Carter uncapped one of the miniatures as she knotted the napkin around his neck. "You'll find steak and eggs on the tray as well."

"First things first." He sipped from the small bottle, letting the liquid jolt him the rest of the way into the world of the living.

Finished with the napkin, Ginger uncapped the other miniature, poured it into a glass, and took a chair near the bed.

"The tape Mayflower dictated is transcribed."

"And?" Carter asked, attacking the food.

"Dynamite."

"How so?"

"It's too involved. Hawk is already making preparations for you to head 'em off at the pass."

Carter made a face. "When does he want me?"

"As soon as you're up and around with the kinks out."

The Killmaster sighed. "An agent's work is never done."

Ginger finished her drink and stood. "We've set up temporary planning headquarters in the pool house. The man would like your recuperation within the hour."

"So be it."

Carter watched her leggy stride take her through the door, and set the tray to one side. Then he slid his feet to the floor and got up, slowly, testing his strength.

His head throbbed a little, and both of the wounds still burned, but he was moving. He tried his strength, lifting himself on the backs of two chairs, swinging his body back and forth with feet off the floor. It left him sweaty and trembling, but after a couple of minutes he felt sure enough of his legs to motivate.

A shower was a problem. He settled for an area sponge bath and a shave. Fresh clothes, exactly his size, were laid out on one of the chairs.

He chuckled as he dressed. AXE business was as hard on the wardrobe as it was on the body.

Five minutes later, he was ready for David Hawk and whatever Viktor Prokudin had dictated into the little tape recorder as he lay dying in the back of the Jeep.

"The project is code-named High Dive. It came into being approximately three years ago. At that time, I was serving as communications liaison between the Rome *rezident*, Oleg Grechko, and various KGB controls throughout Europe. As such, fragments and bits and pieces of High Dive came across my desk.

"Basically, High Dive is the following:

"Five top scientists in five different countries around the world had begun pooling information on their individual space research. This went on for over two years. Eventually, each of these scientists realized that, individually, they each had the master key to unlocking the riddle of an affordable space station.

"By 'space station,' each of these people meant a platform in space whereby further exploration of space could be achieved.

"Needless to say, when our intelligence people learned of this long-range pooling of knowledge—and the progress that had been achieved—there was a great deal of interest.

"How the KGB learned of this I will describe later.

"If a space station could be built inexpensively, and if it could be re-manned and supplied—also inexpensively—and if it could acquire an independent defense system to carry on its work independent of any single power on earth, then these scientists idealistically decided they would automatically have the consummation devoutly to be wished.

"Idealistic, and foolish.

"If such a station could be built, not for space research, but as a launching pad for offensive weapons, whoever controlled it could control the earth.

"High Dive was inaugurated to convince the five scientists that they should meet face-to-face and pool all their knowledge. Once this was done, and the validity of their project actually proven, they could go to private industry in their individual countries and raise the money to build the station.

"Eventually a date and a place was agreed upon. Each of the five would take his holiday at the same time. They would all sail on the twenty-fifth of June aboard the *Grecian Mist* out of Miami, Florida. The cruise would last twenty days. In that time, all the knowledge from each of the five would be pooled.

"None of the five scientists' employers, be they government or private industry, would know of the meeting. By doing it this way, they thought that they could maintain control.

"What four of them didn't know was that the fifth member of their group was a Soviet sympathizer.

"Following are the names and brief biographical sketches of the five.

"Sherman Longtree, an American. For several years he was head of NASA's supersecret 'Space Probe.' When the project folded because of a lack of funds, Longtree left NASA and went into business for himself as a consultant. Besides being considered one of the foremost experts on space propulsion and energy conversion, Longtree is a brilliant economist. It was decided that it would be Longtree who would raise the private funding for the station and act as its first chairman.

"Hallam Dalton is a British citizen, and has long been in the forefront of laser research and the creation of new, lightweight alloys for space flight.

"Guntar Schimmer is a doctor of physics at Heidelburg University. His father, Hermann, was one of the chief scientists behind Hitler's V-one and V-two projects. He is an expert in space architecture.

"Georges Pinot, a Frenchman, is considered the father of the space shield, a defense shield using the vacuum of space to form the impregnable defense system.

"Dr. Fiora Valanotti is a psychologist. The actual running of the station, and literally creating a city or a colony in space, would be her job.

"There you have it. Four men and one woman who, combined, have the knowledge to give the Soviet Union the ultimate weapon of aggression.

"When Grechko was transferred from Rome to Mexico City, I was naturally sent with him. For several months I saw nothing pertaining to High Dive. Then, a few weeks ago, questions began pouring into Mexico City for Grechko's advice.

"Valdik Bessedovsky had become the new *rezident* in Rome after Grechko's departure. As such, he had inherited the control of High Dive.

"Colonel Bessedovsky is a large slob of a man who has spent his entire career doing things by the book. While he is not stupid, he is also not very creative. The intrigues of

High Dive were too much for him without Grechko's help.

"For the last week before my defection I tried to find out the plan for the culmination of High Dive, and the identity of the Soviet agent.

"I hope I have succeeded.

"The agent's code name is Volga.

"After accumulating all the intelligence possible, Volga will defect in one of the Black Sea ports called on by the *Grecian Mist*.

"Just before I met Carter, I was able to get the computer key-code that would give me access to the High Dive file. Under the code name Volga was listed the West German's name: Guntar Schimmer.

"Good luck."

Carter dropped the typewritten sheets on the coffee table before him, and rubbed his eyes. Across from him, the tweedy bulk of David Hawk, his head wreathed in blue smoke from his habitual cigar, was leaning forward. He filled Carter's cup with hot coffee and spoke around the cigar.

"I think you'll have to take a cruise."

"Why?" Carter asked, lighting a cigarette before lifting the cup. "Why don't we just detain Longtree and notify Germany, Italy, France, and the U.K. to take care of their own?"

Hark shook his head. "On what grounds? You think the words of a dead defector who, when it came down to it, was working for money, is enough weight for that?"

Carter sipped the coffee. What Hawk said was true. Prokudin could have been creating the whole thing for a last big payment before he flew. There was a good chance the countries involved wouldn't buy it. Especially with such prominent people involved.

"We can't stop anybody from taking a vacation, Nick,"

Hawk continued, "ours or theirs. Also, there is bound to be a certain amount of embarrassment about this going on for so long and no one knowing anything about it."

"Except the Russians," Carter said dryly.

"Except the Russians," Hawk agreed grimly. "And from the report you dictated this morning, we can't move on just Guntar Schimmer."

Carter nodded. He knew that Hawk was alluding to the fact that Prokudin might have been blown before he got into the High Dive master file. That was pretty evident from the blanks in the gun they had given Prokudin.

Carter stretched and sighed. "So you want me to sail on the *Grecian Mist*."

Hawk nodded. "Looks like it's the only way. Somehow you'll have to get close to the German and satisfy, in your own mind, that he is Volga."

"And if I do?"

"Do you have to ask, Nick? If what Prokudin says is true, the combined knowledge of those five brains can't get to Moscow intact."

"And if Guntar Schimmer isn't Volga, you want me to find out who is."

Hawk worried his cigar. "Asking a lot, isn't it? But you should have some hints. We've gone over background on every one of the five. It's there, in that folder. We know when they took their first step as babies way back when, and we know the color of their underwear, and the brand of toothpaste they use right now. Hopefully, through on-the-spot observation, something will tip you."

"Hopefully," Carter said, carrying his coffee cup to a portable bar. He laced the coffee with a generous splash of whiskey before turning and speaking again. "I go alone?"

"Yes, but we've managed to get two of our people on the crew for backup. Sylvia Liebstrum will be working with the cruise director's people. That will put her in a position to hear things."

Carter grunted. He had worked with Sylvia before. She was young, but good. "Who else?"

"Ray Hooper. We got him into the ship's radio shack. He'll try to get a wire into Schimmer's cabin. That should make it a little easier for you."

"Are they all traveling solo?"

Hawk picked up a sheet of paper from the coffee table and ran his eye down the list. "The Italian woman, Valanotti, is traveling alone. Pinot, the Frenchman, is also alone. Longtree's wife, Joann, is accompanying him. Hallam Dalton has a secretary he travels with all the time. Her name is Monica Sims."

"She travels everywhere with him? Mistress?"

"Chances are good, yes. Dalton is the youngest of the five. He's kind of a boy genius, and according to our reports, he's randy as hell, quite a ladies' man."

"What about the German, Schimmer?"

"Here's where we might have a connection. Schimmer is married, but he's going on the cruise alone. It seems his wife is a mental case. She's in a sanitarium in East Germany."

"*East* Germany?" Carter said.

"Seems they've been separated for some time. She was evidently from the East in the first place. When they separated, she went back. That was before she went bonkers."

"So Schimmer is alone?"

"In a way." Hawk replied. "Seems he and the Italian woman went to school together, had a bit of an affair. Lately it appears to have been rekindled. They've arranged to have adjacent staterooms on the ship."

"My God," Carter groaned, "it's a soap opera."

"Maybe, but it could be a deadly one." Hawk stood,

buttoning his jacket. "You'll be on the A-level deck, first class. That puts you right in the middle of them. Good luck, Nick."

"I'll need it."

"And one more thing..." Hawk pulled a folded slip of paper from his jacket and dropped it on the table in front of Carter. "No one has seen this except me ... and now you. If you decide to do nothing about it, give it back to me. If you decide to do something about it, I've never seen it."

Hawk walked out of the room and Carter stared at the folded slip of paper. It was smeared with blood, and Carter knew it was the same paper that had been in Viktor Prokudin's hand when he died.

He picked it up, avoiding the dried blood, and unfolded it:

Carter:
I've made a right botch of it, I'm afraid. Hope the tape gives you enough to go on. If it does, then I've "earned my keep," as you Americans say. I think I will also have earned what I've already collected.

In the Suiss Europa Nationale in Zurich, there is nearly two million dollars. The bank account number is ALW 9191900. The signature name is J. J. Jordan, and the identifying code is EX LIBRIS.

The co-signer on the account is in Vienna, Number 27, Borse Gasse, just inside the Ring. Her name is Alexis Brondosky. She has twin daughters. The daughters are an indiscretion of my youth that I planned on making right once I had my freedom.

It is my last wish that you put Alexis together with Zurich.

Viktor

Carter stubbed out his cigarette and finished the laced coffee. He stared out across the swimming pools through the trees to the lights of Veracruz, and he thought about the eight ulcer-making years Viktor Prokudin had gone through.

Then he memorized the pertinent information on the note, placed it in the ashtray, and touched the flame of his lighter to one corner.

When it was just ashes, he picked up the file on the five scientists and walked from the room.

TEN

The sitting room of the suite was on the hotel's fourteenth floor. The large window had an unobstructed view of Pier 14, the *Grecian Mist* at dockside, and the open gangway leading from the exterior into the ship's starboard side amidships.

Mounted at the window were two powerful telescopes.

Near one of the scopes, Ivan Yegerov smoked a cigarette. Behind Yegerov, lounging at the bar with a drink in his hand, was Evor Lundesburg. He was a tall, blond-haired, blue-eyed, barrel-chested Swede. He had been recruited by the KGB First Directorate at the age of eighteen while on a sight-seeing trip to Moscow. Since that time, Lundesburg had committed fourteen murders for his KGB chiefs all around the globe.

Pacing between the two men was the woman that Dr. Everett Ellis knew as Lenore Bonstedt. She looked especially attractive today in a pair of slim slacks and a lightweight sweater that outlined her full breasts.

It was her job, as part of the team, to look good. She would play the role of Lundesburg's spouse aboard the *Grecian Mist*.

The fourth occupant of the room was standing at the other telescope. He had not moved his eye from the glass since the boarding had begun an hour earlier.

His name was Armando Cruz, and he was a doctor in a

small Mexican village. Yegerov had brought him to Miami from Mexico City the previous evening.

"Nothing?" the Russian asked.

"Nothing so far," the Mexican doctor replied. "None of the men even resemble him."

The woman spoke, agitation in her voice. "What if they don't send the same agent who got Prokudin out?"

"Then, my dear," Lundesburg quipped, "you will have to seduce every male passenger on the ship until you discover which one it is."

"Oh, shut up, you ass," she retorted.

"Quiet, both of you!" Yegerov barked.

The Swede shrugged and smiled and freshened his drink. Very little bothered him in life. He was a man without joy and without sorrow. He lived for one thing, to kill people.

The woman turned from the window and walked to a chair, sat down, and crossed her legs. Her fine features, normally characterized by their composure, were now taut. Tension showed in the tightness of her pale, pink lips. She snatched a cigarette from the table beside her, lit it, and puffed nervously.

They were asking too much of her. Her mission had been to seduce the ship's doctor, Ellis. She hadn't achieved that, but she had lured him to the Morris House suite so that Stavanger could beat him until Ellis agreed to take their man as his assistant on the cruise.

Now they were asking her to go again on the same cruise. It was too dangerous. Some of the ship's crew would remember her. That weak-livered fat doctor would be frightened and give her away.

She was afraid.

She looked up at Lundesburg's cold eyes and bland smile, and shivered.

That would be the worst part of it. For as long as she was on the ship, she would have to share a cabin with the Swede. Just his presence made her sweat with fear.

"That's him!" the Mexican cried. "The one with the small blue bag and the green blazer!"

Yegerov bent to his own glass. "You're sure?"

"Positive. It took me nearly an hour to treat his two wounds. I wouldn't forget him."

Yegerov motioned the Swede and the woman to the window. "Look at him. Memorize his face."

As they were doing that, Yegerov ran to the bedroom window. Quickly, he ran the venetian blind up and down twice.

On the A-level deck, a huge bear of a man with a mane of black hair saw the venetian blind go up and down, and dived for the ladder well. Seconds later he appeared at the opening below, just behind the purser checking the passengers aboard.

When the man in the green blazer carrying the small blue bag had passed through, he returned to the rail on the A-level deck. He lit a cigarette, took two deep drags, and flipped it into the sea.

Yegerov returned to the sitting room. "Horst has the name he's using, and the cabin number. Did you both get a good look at him?" The Swede and the woman nodded. "Then get aboard."

Without a word, the man and woman left the suite. Yegerov turned to the Mexican. "Congratulations, Doctor."

Cruz shrugged. "I do what I can for the cause. We leave now?"

Yegerov nodded. "We have a twelve-ten flight to Mexico City. A car will be waiting. You will be back in your village by this evening."

* * *

Carter smiled with satisfaction when he stepped into the stateroom. It was made up of a decent-sized bedroom, a sitting room, and a luxurious bath. Every convenience, including a well-stocked minibar, was provided.

Traveling in luxury was one of the perks of the job. All one had to do to get them was be shot at, sometimes tortured, kill people, and live on the cutting edge every minute, twenty-four hours a day.

All in all, Carter thought, *not a bad life.*

He unpacked the wardrobe Bateman had packed for him in the two large bags, and then set out his shaving gear and the rest from the small, blue flight bag.

From a false bottom of the flight bag he lifted an adhesive-sided leather case. In the case was his stiletto, Hugo, and 9mm Luger, Wilhelmina, a silencer for same, and two extra loaded clips of 9mm ammunition. For this trip he had included an over-and-under Colt Derringer, thin as a deck of cards and able to fire .38 hollow-points.

Using the screwdriver on his Swiss army knife, he removed the vent lid in the bathroom. Into the vent, as far as he could reach, went the leather case. Minus the plastic coating over the adhesive, it held solid to the side of the vent.

When the cover was replaced, he removed his shirt and tie, replaced them with a lightweight turtleneck, and headed for the promenade deck.

The big cruise ship was already moving, the skyline of Miami and the jumble of hotels and high-rise condos of Miami Beach falling away.

He paused at the lounge, got a drink to travel with, and moved back out to the deck. After waving their good-byes from the rail, the passengers were already starting to settle in. Several had claimed deck chairs and were already into the romance novels or Dick Francis mysteries that would occupy them for the next twenty days. Others were heading toward the lounges, while some just strolled. One woman with hair that looked like blue wire was in a warmup suit doing laps around the deck.

Carter moved with the flow, nodding, smiling, fielding interested glances from the single women, and keeping alert for the members of what he had personally dubbed the "High Dive Crew."

He was nearing the stern on the promenade deck, the part that overlooked the outdoor café and the pool on the veranda deck below, when he spotted three of them together.

The American, Sherman Longtree, sat in a chrome wheelchair. He was emaciated and gaunt, and his face had a pallor beneath thin gray hair. He was wearing an open-throated sport shirt, and there was a coverlet over his wasted legs.

His wife, Joann, sat in a deck chair close beside him, holding his hand. She was a tiny woman. Her white hair, stringy and thin, was combed back and put up in a meager bun. She had a kindly, perpetually smiling face with thin, bloodless lips and bright eyes surrounded by many tiny wrinkles.

They were both listening intently to a tall, striking woman who lounged with her back to the rail. The woman was Fiora Valanotti, and as Carter examined her out of the corner of his vision, he could see why her co-workers had dubbed her the "Dark Sexy Dragon Lady."

In figure-fitting black slacks and an equally tight black top, she looked both sexy and ominous. She was well past forty, but trim, with a flat belly and high, thrusting breasts. Her hair was long and jet black, and worn severely combed

back with a part in the middle, the classic fashion so familiar on ballerinas. Her hazel eyes were shadowed, but clear
and direct. Even though she talked in quick, staccato sen-
tences and—like most Italians—used her hands for emphasis, there wasn't a trace of animation in her face.

Even from a distance, Carter could sense the aura of
strength that hovered around her. Fiora Valanotti was a
woman to be reckoned with.

Carter had no interest in their conversation at the moment, so he continued his tour. Below, at the bar behind
the veranda café, he paused to refresh his drink. As it was
being poured, he got lucky again.

Georges Pinot, the Frenchman, and the Brit, Hallam
Dalton, were standing at the opposite end of the bar in
deep conversation.

They made quite a pair.

Dalton fit his dossier. He was well tailored, full-mus-
cled, with a sleek, smooth face and an eye that was taking
in every bikini at the pool.

Looking closer, Carter realized that the muscles were
just a little too thick, making the fit of the clothes a hair
wrong. The handsome face had just a bit of a jowl, and the
patent-leather hair was slicked straight back in a fashion
that had passed its prime.

On the other hand, Georges Pinot oozed his Frenchness.
Nearing sixty, he didn't show it. Slim and elegant, he wore
a Continental tailored suit with tight-fitting trousers, a
jacket contoured in the Italian style, and a magenta silk
foulard artfully tucked into the neck of his pale blue shirt.

The barman brought Carter's drink. He was about to go
in search of the rest of the band, when a dark-haired
woman joined the two men. She kissed Dalton lightly on
the cheek, and Carter strained to hear the introductions. He

was slightly surprised when he realized that this was the one member of the group of whom there had been no photo in the background material he received from Hawk.

It was Dalton's secretary-cum-mistress, Monica Sims, and somehow she didn't fit the image that Carter had conjured up for the Englishman's choice in women.

Unlike practically every other woman on the ship, she wasn't dressed to expose her better features. In fact, she wore a simple, long-sleeved sweater with a turtleneck that reached to her chin. Her skirt was plain, too, and there was nothing special about her low-heeled, sensible shoes. She dressed as though she were deliberately trying to avoid attention. Carter even had a hunch that her bra was selected to hold in her ample breasts.

It was her face that defeated any effort to gain anonymity. Devoid of makeup, it was striking rather than beautiful, and almost stern. It was set off by shoulder-length dark brown hair with just a touch of the unkempt look.

Carter strained to hear the conversation, but the chatter in between blotted it out. About the only thing he learned before he moved on was a bit more about the relationship between Dalton and secretary/mistress.

The Frenchman, Pinot, was making obvious overtures to the woman, who was, just as obviously, accepting them. Dalton just as obviously spotted it, but he continued to check out the action around the pool.

Maybe, Carter thought, *Hawk's intelligence may have missed the boat on this pair. Perhaps Monica Sims was just a secretary, nothing more.*

He cruised the teakwood decks for another half hour, but he couldn't spot the German, Schimmer.

He was pleased to find, when he returned to his stateroom, that it had been searched thoroughly and professionally. Nothing was out of place, not even the fine hairs he had placed around.

But the faint aroma in the air was perfume, not his shaving lotion. Also, the slight indentations on the newly vacuumed bathroom rug were made by narrow, sharp heels, not the wide, flat heels of the maid's shoes or those worn by the steward.

In a pair of beige slacks, stripped to the waist, Evor Lundesburg did push-ups in the center of the room. The muscles of his arms and back were like corded hemp beneath the tanned skin.

A television was on in one corner. Near it, Lenore hovered, one eye on the screen, the other on the Swede. In front of her lay a spread of sandwiches, fruit, and coffee, all untouched.

There was a single knock on the door and Lundesburg was off the floor like a cat. Horst Stavanger squeezed his bulk through the crack in the door and the Swede closed it behind him. In spite of the air conditioning, the big, black-haired man was sweating profusely. He spotted the food in front of Lenore and moved toward it.

"Yours?"

She nodded. "I lost my appetite watching Mr. Universe here."

Stavanger chuckled, took a stool, and began shoveling food into his mouth.

The Swede scowled at the woman and took the empty stool. "Well?"

"He's our man, all right. I watched him make his way around the ship. He made each one of them."

"Lenore found nothing in his stateroom," the Swede said.

"His passport was not altered," she added. "It was genuine."

Stavanger laughed. Food dribbled down his chin, making the woman avert her eyes. "Of course his passport was genuine. He's American! It was probably issued by the U.S. State Department. What was listed as his occupation?"

"Journalist," she replied.

"Any arms?"

"No," she said, shaking her head, "none."

Stavanger drank the cup of coffee in one slurping swallow and refilled the cup. "He was not armed on his person, either. I'm sure of it."

The Swede smiled, putting his hands together and making the powerful muscles in his arms go taut. "I'll put him overboard tonight!"

"No," Stavanger replied, wiping his mouth and chin on his sleeve. "We'll wait, perhaps until Tangier."

"Why?"

"To see if he has taken the bait on Schimmer. If he has, his superiors also have. We may not have to kill him. In the meantime, Lenore, see what you can do with him. He has first service for dinner. The table is B-sixty-one. That would be a good place to start."

She nodded.

Stavanger downed the second cup of coffee and moved to the door. "I will try to get a photograph of this Nicholas Stevens. When we get to Tangier, I will have it sent to Moscow to see if he is in the files. In the meantime, we observe."

He checked the passageway and slipped out.

"God," the woman grunted in disgust.

"What?" the Swede asked.

"Him, Stavanger. He's such a slob!"

The Swede's eyebrows met in a vee. She was right. Horst Stavanger was a good agent, but he was a slob. This was not a good assignment for the East German.

On board the *Grecian Mist,* in the midst of such glittering, beautiful people, he stuck out . . . far out.

ELEVEN

It was midafternoon. Carter had just changed into a pair of swimming trunks and a pullover when she knocked. He had planned on some further reconnaissance by the pool before the evening meal.

It wasn't to be.

"Hello, Mr."—she glanced down at the clipboard in her hand and back up with a beaming smile—"Stevens?"

That's right . . ."

"I'm Sylvia. Welcome aboard the *Grecian Mist*. I'm your entertainment coordinator, and I'm here to see that you enjoy your trip. Now, we have a steady round of physical fitness activities, brain-teasing quizzes, bingo games, films, and dance classes . . ."

She kept chattering as she moved into the room, and Carter closed the door. He listened to make sure no one had popped up on the other side, and turned to face her.

Sylvia Liebstrum was what is called an "outdoor girl," with a sturdy and well-shaped body, and a square but very attractive face. Her long dark brown hair was pulled back in a braid. She had hazel eyes in a tanned, earnest face. Her mouth might have been too broad, but she showed fine teeth when she laughed. If she was not exactly pretty, health and vigor gave her a strong attractiveness which was better than that.

She was still going on. ". . . so if activity is your desire, there's an entire ship's staff ready to support and serve you—"

He shut her up by kissing her. "Hello, Sylvia," he said with a grin.

"Hi, Nick, good to see you again."

"I love your uniform."

"Awful, isn't it? I look like a choir boy in drag!"

"How's the job?" he chuckled.

"Awful. How do people stand it? Do you know, my boss is thirty-eight and she's been doing this for fifteen years!"

Carter lit a cigarette and guided her to the large, comfortable sofa. "What about your other job?"

She fumbled with the clipboard and came up with a map and several pieces of paper, some typed, some computer printouts.

"Here's the passenger list. It's almost a sure thing that Volga will have a backup on board. Washington hasn't had time to go through them all, so we'll have to wait until Tangier to get a complete rundown."

"Tangier?"

She nodded. "That's our first port of call. The man seems to think that if *we* got two people onto the ship's staff, they might be able to do the same."

"So the ship's regular channels of communication might be risky."

"You got it."

"So when's Tangier?"

She spread the sailing map out between them on the couch. The ports of call were in heavy red and joined with dark broken lines. "Seven days," she replied.

"Seven days?" Carter exploded. "My God, anything can happen in seven days!"

"Well," Sylvia shrugged, "let's hope most of it happens for *our* side."

Quickly, she ran through the ports of call: Catania, Sicily, after Tangier, then Santorini, Greece, and Kusadasi, Turkey. She also gave him land contacts for each one. Carter already knew most of them and said so. "After Kusadasi, it's Istanbul and the Russian Black Sea ports."

"And that's where Volga says bye-bye," Carter said. "My guess is Savastopol. It's the last Black Sea stop. Volga will want the time to get all the intelligence possible."

"That makes sense," Sylvia replied. "It also makes sense that Istanbul will be the tip-off."

"Let's hope," Carter said, "that we blow Volga quicker than Istanbul. What else have you got?"

Another slip of paper. "This is a copy of all the stateroom numbers. As you know, Schimmer and Valanotti are adjoining. The others are nearby. They have also requested, paid extra for, and received permission from the chief steward for use of the Nomad Room for the entire cruise."

"Conferences, most likely."

"Most likely," she agreed. "They claim it's an ongoing poker game along with some business talks."

"That would fit. According to their sheets, Dalton and Longtree both fancy themselves world-class gamblers. Any chance for Roy Hooper to get a wire into the room?"

"You'll have to ask him yourself. We've been careful to stay apart. It would be difficult for us to get together, anyway. Believe it or not, there is a tremendous class distinction among the crew. Roy is electronic and communications maintenance, I'm topside. They don't mix."

"What do you think?"

"My guess is, no. The Nomad Room is far forward and topside, near the bridge. There are no electronics in the room, not even a television set, so there's no reason for Roy to go in there. It's heavily locked at all times when it's not in use."

"Okay, what about Schimmer's stateroom?"

"Again, you'll have to ask Hooper. When I leave, call maintenance. Tell them that the picture is clouding on your TV. Hopefully, Roy will take the call. He's watching for it."

"Good. It looks like we'll be playing cat and mouse with the backup team."

"How so?"

"While I was making the grand tour, someone checked out my stateroom. A woman."

"You're sure?"

"Positive," he said. "I don't wear perfume. The place reeked with it when I got back. By the way, did you keep tabs on me?"

"I did, until you got to the lower decks. Down there it would have been obvious that I was following you."

"Anything?"

"Lots"—Sylvia smiled mischievously—"and all women. These cruise ships are four-to-one women. A single man doesn't go unnoticed or unappreciated. I made a list of those who took a *lot* of interest, but . . ."

"Yeah," Carter said, "if a woman was going through my stateroom, it was probably a man who was casing me on deck. By the way, I spotted everyone but Schimmer."

Sylvia laughed. "That's because he was seasick. He took to his cabin the moment the ship got underway."

"Seasick?"

"That's what the ship's doctor told me. Dr. Ellis gave him a couple of shots right after we sailed."

"That's odd . . ."

"Oh?"

"According to Prokudin, Volga was the one who promoted the cruise as a place for the five of them to have their conferences. If Volga is Schimmer, it seems odd that he would choose the sea if he's susceptible to seasickness. Pump this Dr. Ellis and find out how serious the seasickness was . . . if it was real."

"Will do." Sylvia stood, straightening her cute little blue skirt. "Anything else for now?"

Carter stood and tilted her face with a finger under the chin. "Yeah. When do I see you again?"

"When do you want to see me again?" she whispered.

He was about to say "Midnight," then thought better of it. He remembered Fiora Valanotti standing at the rail, and the scent of perfume in his stateroom. He guessed that, with a woman involved, it would be better to keep his options open.

"I guess I'd better just call you if I decide to sign up for dancing lessons."

Her lips started to form a little pout and then she thought better of it. "You're right. We're instructed not to spend too much time with any one passenger. I'll get anything I uncover back to you by folding it in your copy of the ship's newspaper. It's delivered every morning."

Carter nodded his agreement as she opened the door.

"So, Mr. Stevens, don't forget . . . you can call on us for anything. Have a good time!"

Then she was gone and Carter was reaching for the phone.

A male voice answered at once. "Maintenance."

"Yes, this is Mr. Stevens on the sky deck, suite one-fourteen . . ."

"Yes, sir?"

"My television is snowy. At these prices, I want the bloody thing fixed and I want it done straight away!"

"Yes, sir, right away, sir."

Carter hung up and built himself a drink.

Faintly, just faintly, he could still smell the perfume. Sylvia had also been wearing perfume, but it was light, barely noticeable.

This scent was heavy, permeating.

He was sure that when he encountered it again, he would know it.

The dining room steward was a solidly built man with iron gray-hair who moved his bulk with an easy grace. He spotted the tall, beautiful blonde the moment she stepped through the door.

He encountered so many people on each cruise, it was difficult to remember. But this one, with her marvelous figure and that hair . . . this one he remembered.

The name? No. But that face and figure he wouldn't forget.

"Madam, may I help you?"

"Yes, I understand you're the dining room steward."

His eyes widened in surprise, but he covered it with a toothy smile. He almost said, "Of course I'm the chief steward. You know that from the last cruise barely two weeks ago!"

But instead he said, "Yes, madam."

"I am Mrs. Lundesburg. I'd like to know our seating arrangements for dinner."

"Of course." He flipped through his seating charts, found the name, and looked up. "*Mrs*. Lundesburg?"

"Yes."

He blinked. What he did remember was that she had been alone on the last cruise. He was sure of it. "Of course. You and your husband are second seating, table J-nineteen."

"Oh, dear, that just won't do. I must have first seating. My husband is adamant about first serving."

"That will be no problem, Mrs. Lundesburg. Let me see . . . ah. There is space available during first seating at L-seventeen."

"L-seventeen," she murmured, casting her eye around the huge, domed room with its immaculate white linen in place and presided over by six enormous, glittering chandeliers. "Where would that be?"

"This way, madam."

He led her to a choice table. It was only three down from the captain's table, and directly beside a huge window with a striking view of the starboard side of the ship and the ocean beyond.

"No, no, this won't do, either. My husband can't stand looking out on that while he's dining. He has a bit of seasickness, you know."

Your husband, madam, is an ass, he thought. But before he could inquire just what would please her fussy spouse, she was off through the tables.

"Here, this would be fine!"

He consulted his clipboard. "I am sorry, madam, but B-sixty-one is full, eight people, for first seating."

Her hand flashed forward and grasped his. He had been a dining room steward for fifteen years. When her hand left his, he knew the feel of crisp, folded bills in his palm.

"I'm sure you can make the adjustment," she purred.

Then she was gone.

With thumb and forefinger, he unfolded the bills and looked down. There were three crisp, American hundred-dollar bills in his hand.

Oh, yes, he thought, with such enticement he was sure he could make the adjustment.

He was back at his station, penciling in the change,

when he remembered. Slightly different method on the last cruise, but now he was sure it was the same woman.

On the last cruise it had also been three hundred dollars, but it had been sent down to him from her stateroom in an envelope.

At that time, she had requested one of the places at a staff table, the one with the ship's doctor, Everett Ellis.

Roy Hooper was a bulky man of medium height, with a bristling mustache and eyes that were keen and alert behind thick-lensed glasses. Despite his bulk, he moved springily with the gait of an outdoorsman.

His greetings to Carter were terse, and he went right to work on the television. Once the back panels were off, his fingers fairly flew. Wires were disconnected and reconnected in different ways. A black box about half the size of a cigar box was cleverly engineered into the TV, and more wires were connected.

Finally, with everything back in place, he motioned Carter over.

"Schimmer's cabin is only two away from yours. That's good, because the oscillating power on the bug I planted isn't very powerful. The good part about that is, it's practically undetectable without some pretty fancy equipment. That type of equipment would be too bulky for him to bring aboard."

Carter nodded. "How do I work my end?"

"Simple." Hooper unhinged the side of the box. It opened, and inside Carter saw a cassette receptacle similar to those in automobiles, only much smaller. From his pocket, Hooper produced a minicassette about one-inch-by-two. *"Voilà."*

"What's the length?" Carter asked.

"Four hours, two on a side. It's sound-activated, so

you'll go through tapes pretty fast. Got a place you can secure these? You just might need them all."

He handed Carter a bound package of ten tapes. The Killmaster took them and nodded. "Is the playback in there as well?"

"It is, if you need it, utilizing the television speakers. But you might miss something while you're playing back, so I brought you this."

It was a small recorder/playback unit similar to those used by businessmen away from their desks for dictation.

"Any switches?"

"Just close the lid. The two clamps activate. This little light will come on blue when you've got a half-hour left. It goes red when the tape's out."

"Good enough."

The rear cover on the television was replaced, and Hooper built himself a drink from the minibar.

"I got a look at the Italian. She's a lot of woman, Nick. For my money, if the German isn't Volga, she is."

The Killmaster splashed more scotch into his own glass and nodded in agreement. "I've been thinking the same thing. Let's hope the tape gives us more to go on. Now, what about this Nomad Room, where they plan on holding their meetings?"

"Checked it out. No way. It's bare. Anything that goes in, they bring themselves. The room is sterile. It's designed that way to stop any industrial espionage. You'd be surprised how many high-powered corporations choose cruise ships to get their business done."

"Okay," Carter replied, "we'll settle for what we've got and hope for the best. Have you circulated with the crew?"

"Yeah, and, frankly, I can't fit any one of 'em into Volga's backup. Besides myself, there are only two who haven't been with the line for a long time, and they don't fit."

"Sylvia says the same thing about the topside staff. Anyway, I'd guess the backup would be passengers. Did you bring hardware aboard?"

Hooper nodded. "Enough to start a war if we need it."

"Let's hope we don't," Carter said. "How do I get you if I need to?"

"Same way you did just now. Cheers!"

Hooper emptied his glass and headed for the door.

Carter checked his watch, decided against the pool, and began to change for the first evening meal at sea.

TWELVE

Carter drew a real royal flush for tablemates at B61.

To his left was Mrs. Bernstein, in overflowing green satin and a half ton of jewelry. Her dear husband, Mr. Bernstein the wholesale jeweler, had passed on six years earlier. Since that time, Mrs. Bernstein had cruised all the way around the world five times, stopping back at her New York apartment only long enough to deposit her dividend checks and kiss her poodles.

To her left were the Borly sisters, retired schoolteachers from Dubuque. The cruise was their retirement gift to each other. Kitty Borly was an elephant in stripes, and Alice was an aging Twiggy in stripes before Twiggy got smart and gained weight.

Neither of them talked, but they giggled a lot and whispered to each other.

To Carter's right were the Gattlings. They hailed from Denver, where Harold Gattling was in oil and anything else that made money.

Harold was a plumpish man with a bright red suntan and thinning hair bleached by too much sun. He wore a trendy tux with so many ruffles he wouldn't be able to see his food when it arrived.

Harold's wife, Juanita, was a lush. She was attractive, with long straight red hair parted in the middle. Her dress was gold patio pajamas, and she drank straight gin and directed bitchy put-downs at everything her husband said.

Carter ordered scotch and tried to look comfortable. By the time the drink came, he wished he had ordered a double.

"Fertilizer," Harold Gattling was saying, "that's the thing now. Get set up right and you can make a fortune."

Carter smiled dumbly and nodded, wondering who belonged to chairs seven and eight across from him.

Evidently, Mrs. Gattling felt she had to explain her husband's position. She got a vise grip on Carter's leg, swayed in his direction, and breathed lethal alcohol fumes in his face when she spoke. "Harold's big on shit."

The smell of gin was powerful in his nostrils, but even more powerful was the heavy musk on her perfume. He was about to comment on it, when the Lundesburgs arrived.

The men stood and were introduced by the chief dining room steward.

"Stocks," Evor Lundesburg replied in answer to Harold Gattling's query.

"Swede, huh?"

Lundesburg nodded. So did his attractive wife, Lenore. But both their eyes kept glancing at Carter.

Lundesburg was quite a specimen, a man who obviously took good care of his body. Not that his wife didn't. She wore a halter-necked dress that clung in all the right places and had diamond cutouts around the midriff that revealed a deep, glowing tan. In fact, it looked as though her whole body was deeply tanned.

She seemed to pay a great deal of attention to Carter, but, at the moment, the Killmaster was more interested in Juanita's scent.

He managed to get her attention, but before he could inquire about her perfume, which now seemed stronger than ever, the table was besieged by waiters and wine stewards.

Harold Gattling took over. He held long, esoteric consultations with them all. He buried his nose in the hors d'oeuvres, and pronounced them fit for the human consumption. He debated over the temperature of the water in which the lobster would be cooked. He asked how long the chef simmered his stock for the bouillabaise. For a topper, he ended up ordering wine for the table, a Spanish white, his treat.

Juanita breathed in Carter's ear. "My husband is an asshole."

Carter smiled in agreement and ordered another drink.

During the meal, Carter was taken over by Mrs. Bernstein.

"Do you gamble?"

"Now and then."

"I love it. Abe, that was my husband, Abe would never let me gamble. Said it was a waste of money. How's about you and me hitting the casino after dinner . . . honey?"

Oh, God, Carter thought, and stooped so low as to attack the Spanish white.

Just before dessert, Juanita knocked over a glass of wine and accused Harold of having pushed her elbow. They squabbled like two children, and eventually she stalked from the dining room.

Carter noticed that her scent lingered long after she was gone.

Carter did hit the casino with Mrs. Bernstein. She did love to gamble, and she did it terribly. But it totally absorbed her. Within an hour, he was able to slip away without bothering to make excuses.

In the ballroom, a band was playing slower tunes from

the swing era. At the bar he ordered and eyeballed the room.

The dance floor was a sea of glittering dresses, tuxedos, and gray hair. He spotted Harold Gattling dancing with an attractive woman only a few years his senior. She wore a silk jersey floor-length gown that clung to her like a second skin, and was split from the neck to the navel, showing off lightly tanned skin and an enormous bosom.

She appeared to be in the same inebriated state that Gattling's wife had been at dinner. His hands were kneading her buttocks, and each time he squeezed she roared with laughter.

Then Carter saw them, the "High Dive Crew" minus the Longtrees plus Monica Sims. They were deep in conversation at a corner table well away from the bandstand.

Guntar Schimmer was directly in Carter's sight line. He was a blond, Prussian-looking man of about forty-five. His hair was clipped close to his skull, his face round and rosy-cheeked. Despite a well-fed arrogance, he still looked a little green around the gills.

Carter guessed that his seasickness was for real.

Whatever they were discussing seemed more than just social. Monica Sims was taking notes, and now and then interrupted to ask questions.

"They are a strange lot, are they not, these people who take cruises?"

Carter turned toward the speaker. He was a big man, Carter's height but a good forty pounds over his weight, with a mane of mussed black hair and stains on his tux shirt.

"Yes," Carter replied, "I suppose they are."

"Ah, an American. I am German, but I live in America now. Stavanger, Horst Stavanger."

Carter accepted the offered hand. The grip, casually,

was like a vise. "Nick Stevens. Your first cruise?"

"Yes, I just lost my wife. I thought it would be good to get away. I would like to return to Germany, but a job is a job. Have you ever been to Germany, Herr Stevens?"

Why, Carter thought, *do I feel like this man is weighing me?*

"No. No, I haven't."

"Ah, I have spent a great deal of time in West Berlin. I noticed you at dinner and thought I had seen you before, perhaps even met you."

"No, I'm afraid that would be impossible."

"Oh. I am in textiles. And you?"

"I'm a journalist . . . free-lance."

The men fell silent. They returned their eyes to the room, but every now and then they met in the back bar mirror.

Again Carter felt that the man's eyes were studying him, probing. And in back of their blandness, something stirred. Carter had seen it before. It was contempt.

"If you'll excuse me," Carter said.

"Of course. Nice talking to you."

He meant to pass by the table where the High Dive Crew had congregated, but they had already left. He was skirting through the crowd, when there was a tug at his sleeve.

"Hey, Stevens . . . " It was Harold Gattling.

"Yes, how're you doing, Harold?"

"Great," the man wheezed, a leering grin spread across his face. "I got me a hot one!" He nudged Carter conspiratorially. "She got a friend . . ."

Carter's eyes followed Gattling's nod. Silk-jersey-floor-length waved at them. Beside her, the friend was clad in a black dress that wore the title only by courtesy. She was a short, mushroom-shaped woman who must have weighed every ounce of two hundred pounds. She stared at Carter with frank interest from out of little black shoe-button eyes that, but for their brilliance, must have been lost in the fleshy full moon of her face. Her nose was a mere pink blob, her mouth a plump little circle, her chins three.

"Her name's Lucy," Gattling said. "What do you say?"

"Give Lucy my best, Harold, but I'm a little beat. I think I'll call it a night."

Carter escaped before the man could say another word. He hit the promenade deck and took the long way around to the stairwell that led down to his stateroom. Here he paused, lit a last cigarette, and moved to the rail.

The big white ship was far out on the open sea now, the powerful diesels throbbing steadily beneath the polished decks. The night was warm. The sky was inky black, pierced by thousands of stars that seemed brighter than usual.

He took a last drag on his cigarette and flipped it into the sea. A light breeze caught it and the glow seemed to hold, suspended in the air for a few seconds before it fell and finally disappeared.

Then he tensed, his nostrils flared. That same slight breeze had done something else. It had brought the same, strong musky odor to his nostrils.

"Hello, Mr. Stevens."

The voice came from the deck chair in the semidarkness. It was Mrs. Gattling's voice. Carter moved closer, saw there were two deck chairs pulled side by side, one empty. She reached up to him. Her fingers grabbed his jacket. She pulled him down to her.

"Hello, Mrs. Gattling."

"Would Juanita be too hard to say?" Her words were low, eager, breathless, her voice strange.

Carter's eyes had become a little more used to the darkness. He could see she was wearing a full-length caftan. She moved her arm quickly up around his neck, tugged him over to her, and kissed him frenziedly. For a full minute she clung to him, biting savagely into his lips. There was a strange taste about her mouth: acrid, pungent, warm . . . something Carter couldn't identify. She moved her lips lightly along his jaw, up to the lobe of his ear.

"You're a very attractive man," she whispered.

"I love that perfume," Carter said, inhaling deeply.

"Good! Before we get together again, I'll take a bath in it!"

Carter leaned back. The robe had parted. She wasn't wearing a damn thing beneath it.

"What scent is it?"

She smiled and lowered her eyes in a semblance of sensuality. When she moved toward him slightly, the moonlight danced off her bare breasts. "It's called Jacquelle. It's very expensive, of course, but I gave Horrible Harold a break and bought it at the duty-free shop this afternoon."

"This afternoon?"

"Yes. Let's go . . . to your stateroom."

Her hands headed for his neck again. Carter caught her wrists. "You didn't bring any of this Jacquelle aboard with you? You weren't wearing it this morning?"

"No," she whispered, "but I will from now on."

Carter got to his feet. "Sorry, it's been a long day. I'll see you at breakfast."

Juanita Gattling said nothing, but Carter could feel her icy mood and her eyes burning into his back as he turned into the passageway.

THIRTEEN

It was the fourth day out. So far, Carter had played it laid back. The only change in shipboard routine he had exercised was taking his evening meals for the past two nights in his stateroom. He hadn't felt like idle chitchat with Mrs. Bernstein, and he had become a challenge to Juanita Gattling.

It was bad enough avoiding her in the lounges and on the deck in the daytime. Sitting beside her at the evening meal was just too much.

The tape recording in his television had revealed nothing more about Schimmer than his ardent passion for the Italian woman, Fiora Valanotti, and the fact that both of them were rabid liberals.

According to his daily reports from Sylvia wrapped in the ship's newspaper, the meetings in the Nomad Room were regular and evidently arduous. Twice she had seen them emerge with tired, haggard looks on their faces. Other than the five, Monica Sims was only person in the room while the meetings took place. Sylvia guessed the woman's presence was needed to transcribe what was said.

If this were true, the transcriptions were not kept. According to the cleanup crew, a burn basket was utilized at the end of each day. Also, Sylvia had twice managed to slip into Monica Sims's stateroom and give it a thorough search. There had been no notes or tapes anywhere.

This, Carter thought, seemed to be another oddity in an

already odd situation. If the five of them were meeting to pool their information, and if a secretary was present to record it, where was it recorded?

He himself had done enough snooping to find out that Hallam Dalton was every bit the lover boy of his reputation. Besides sleeping with Sims, he had managed to seduce two of the more attractive women on board, both married and accompanied by their husbands. Monica Sims didn't seem to mind that he went to another woman's bed after leaving hers, or came to hers from another's.

Confusing, but revealing.

One by one, Carter was narrowing down the possibilities for Volga among the five.

He felt Sherman Longtree could be excluded from the running. The man's credentials were just too good, and his personal anti-Communist stand was too strong. Also, his age and the fact of his paralysis would make it difficult to perform as Volga would have to perform.

The Frenchman, Georges Pinot, had been a fair possibility to Carter in the beginning, but after a few casual conversations and a lot of observation, the Killmaster had ruled him out. There were too many little things a trained agent could spot in another trained agent. Carter saw none of them in Pinot.

Hallam Dalton was just what he seemed, a genius with little or no common sense. His sexual athletics and his blind view of the others and himself were too real to be an act. If Dalton were Volga, his superiors would never stand for his laying himself wide open with his teenage-type conquests.

The left Schimmer and Valanotti. At this point, the Killmaster considered one or both of them the prime suspects. Perhaps Schimmer's name hadn't been substituted for another's in the embassy computer. Perhaps he *was*

Volga all along, and Grechko had decided to leave it as is, hoping that American intelligence would automatically figure the switch.

All Carter could do now was keep snooping until they hit the first port of call, Tangier, and see if Washington had unearthed anything new on the five that would provide a ray of sunshine through what was now a very murky situation.

"A chaise, sir?"

"Yes, please, and a gin and tonic."

The deck steward led him to a chaise two rows back from the pool, and departed to fetch the drink. Carter was just settling in when someone sat sidesaddle on the next chaise, blocking out the sun.

"I forgive you."

It was Juanita Gattling with barely a slur in her voice. The drink in her hand was evidently the first of the morning.

"Good morning, Mrs. Gattling."

"Juanita, darlin'. Why didn't you just come right out and tell me the other night that you dug men instead of women?"

That got Carter's attention. Maybe it wasn't her first drink after all. "I beg your pardon?"

"I saw that guy coming out of your stateroom this morning."

"Oh . . . you did?"

"Yeah."

The steward brought Carter's drink. There were two others on the tray, probably for two other people. Juanita helped herself to one of them and waved the man away.

"I saw him open the door to your room and take a good, hard look up and down the passageway before he left."

Carter's mind went over the morning. He had risen

early, before dawn, climbed into a sweat suit, and done a few laps around the deck. Then he had gone in for breakfast without going back to the stateroom. He had been out of his cabin for nearly two hours.

"Tell me, Juanita, what makes you think this gentleman and myself . . . ?" He cut it off there and let his hand do a little wiggle in the air.

She laughed. "Oh, c'mon. At that hour of the morning, what would he be doing in your stateroom if he hadn't spent the night?"

Behind the dark glasses, Carter's eyes narrowed.

"You're right, Juanita, you've found me out."

She shrugged. "To each his own." She put away half the contents of the glass. "But for the life of me I can't see a guy with your looks with such a slob . . ."

Before Carter could find a way to deftly squeeze a description out of her, she was up and away, staggering toward the bar.

"Disgusting, isn't she?"

Carter turned. The chaise to his right was empty. The next one over was occupied by a tall blonde. He didn't recognize her until she moved the sun shield from her face. It was the Swedish woman, Lenore Lundesburg.

"They say chronic drinking is a disease," Carter replied lightly.

"With that woman, it's terminal. You haven't been to dinner the past few nights."

"No, I haven't been feeling well," he said. "Been taking the evening meal in my stateroom. Fact is, I'm not feeling too well right now. Will you excuse me?"

He gathered his towel and cigarettes and headed for the bar. Juanita Gattling had already disappeared.

He headed up to the promenade deck and his stateroom. Carefully, he went over every inch. If someone had searched, he had done one hell of a good job. Carter could detect nothing touched or moved.

The last thing he did was remove the back of the television and check the recorder.

The cassette tape was gone.

Juanita stubbed out her cigarette, and for the tenth time in the last ten minutes checked her watch. Fifteen more minutes. She moved to the bar to fortify herself with just one more gin. She poured and forced herself to sip.

The hell with Nick Stevens, she thought, and to hell with the other men on this whitewashed tub who had given her the cold shoulder and the scornful eye.

He had moved in beside her at the forward lounge during teatime, all six-foot-four, blue-eyed, blond-headed hunk of him.

"We will have to be careful," he had whispered to her through smiling lips. "My wife is extremely jealous. She watches me constantly."

Juanita had been turned on at once. Twice she had offered herself, but he hadn't seemed interested.

"There is an empty stateroom on C deck. A few dollars in the deck steward's pocket and it's ours to use for the evening."

Juanita had suggested they go use it right then, she had been so ready, but he had insisted on meeting on the C-deck observation area of the fantail.

"It is only a few steps to the cabin from there," the handsome Swede had said. "Let's say, when everyone else is just sitting down to first seating? My wife will be occupied, and so will your husband."

"Illicit romance," Juanita said aloud, pouring just one more wee gin. "God, I love it."

She checked herself in a full-length mirror. Her figure in

the clinging dress was ripe. Perhaps even a trifle overripe. She would have to cut down just a little on the gin.

Grabbing a beaded clutch purse, she let herself out of the stateroom. Scarcely any other passengers were about as she made her way down to the lower decks and then aft toward the stern.

The afterdeck was empty when she stepped through the passageway door. Nervously, she moved to the rail, fishing in her purse.

Damn, I've left my case in the stateroom.

A soft padding footstep behind her. She turned, and there he was, stepping out from the shadows of one of the huge vents.

"You came," he said, his husky voice soft with the trace of an accent. "I am so glad."

"Did you have any doubts?" Juanita pursed her lips in what she considered her sexiest look, and let her wrap fall open to reveal the rise of her breasts in the low-cut dress.

God, what an animal he's going to be in bed! she thought, already experiencing the moment when that big, hard body would cover hers.

His hands caressed her hips and tickled up her body to cup the fullness of her breasts. She expanded her lungs, thrusting them willingly into his palms.

She closed her eyes as his lips found hers. Her throat was tight and her chest ached with desire. She spoke while still running her tongue along his lips.

"Where's the stateroom?"

"Soon, my pet," he whispered. "There is no rush, we have time."

With one hand firmly in the small of her back, he withdrew a pint bottle of gin from inside his dinner jacket. He smiled, brushing the tip of her nose with his lips as he unscrewed the cap with thumb and forefinger.

She heard it hit the deck.

"To us," he said, and tipped the bottle to his lips.

When he offered it to her, Juanita grasped it greedily. If she ever needed a drink, she needed it now. Hungrily she took two large swallows, and let the bottle fall to the deck as the hand in the small of her back jerked her roughly to him.

"You are lovely..."

His hands came up to cup the back of her head, fingers touching her neck, threading their way through her hair.

Odd, she thought, *he's wearing some kind of gloves.*

But the thought was pushed from her mind when once again his lips crushed hers. His fingers danced very lightly on the back of her neck, generating waves of pleasurable anticipation through her nervous system.

She moaned and thrust her breasts against him, grinding her hips to his.

His eyes were somber, yet within them she could see the same excitement she felt. He was hers for the night, and whatever she needed from him was hers for the asking.

His fingers stopped with a rippling, massaging motion on her jawline just under her ears. Then he began a sure, slow pressure.

Her breath was suspended. Her lips parted for another kiss, and then they parted farther in a scream.

But no sound came.

She couldn't breathe. The purse slipped from her fingers and fell to the deck. She clawed futilely at the vise that was squeezing the life from her.

She opened her eyes and saw him smiling. Then she struggled one last time, and saw nothing else.

Evor Lundesburg lifted her easily and threw her over the rail. In seconds her body disappeared in the foam and green wake churned up by the ship's props.

Deftly, he peeled the surgical gloves from his hands and threw them over the side.

Leaving the pint bottle of gin with only her fingerprints on it and her purse on the deck, he moved to the ladder-well.

Carter had given up on the perfume. As he seated himself at dinner, the same scent he remembered hovered over the table like a cloud.

Even Mrs. Bernstein reeked of it. He was sure Lenore Lundesburg and the retired schoolteachers were also wearing it. Suddenly, Jacquelle was the rage.

Harold Gattling was being his usual obnoxious self. Carter leaned toward the man when there was a lull in the conversation.

"Your wife isn't dining this evening?"

Harold smiled. "We had a bit of a tiff. She's drinking her dinner in the stateroom."

Carter didn't know the Gattlings' stateroom number, and he couldn't very well come out and ask Harold for it. He would just have to wait until morning and try to catch the woman around the pool drinking her breakfast. He only hoped he could question her and get a description of the man she had seen leaving his stateroom before liquor fogged her memory.

Just as they were ordering, Evor Lundesburg arrived.

"Feeling better, darling?" his wife asked.

"Much," the big Swede replied, and ordered a huge dinner.

Carter stopped in front of his stateroom door and fumbled in his pocket for the key. Suddenly he stiffened. There was a light on in his cabin. He knew he hadn't left it there. Maybe the steward . . . no, they didn't do things that way.

He turned the knob gently, felt the door move slightly. It was unlocked. He gave the door a quick push. It flew open. He stepped inside and looked quickly about.

"Hi."

Sylvia was curled into a corner of the couch sipping a drink. Carter smiled and kicked the door closed behind him, snapping the lock.

"To what do I owe?"

"A couple of tidbits I thought might not wait until morning."

"Speak," he said, pouring himself a brandy.

"I overheard Charles, the dining room steward, talking to his girlfriend. She's the singer in the lounge."

"Yeah?"

"Well, Charles is notorious about gratuities. It's a policy that the stewards get only five percent from the dining room take, as opposed to the waiters' fifteen. Consequently, he plays games with the seating whenever he can, to squeeze a little more out of the passengers."

Carter lit a cigarette and slid in beside her. "And?"

"It seems that on the first afternoon, a woman wanted a certain table so badly that she tipped Charles three hundred dollars. Nick, the table was yours."

A little ripple went up Carter's spine. "The woman?"

"Lenore Lundesburg. And that's not all. Charles swears that this same woman was on the *Grecian Mist* last cruise. She did the same thing then. The table she requested was one of the staff tables."

"Any particular reason?"

Sylvia nodded. "She wanted the table where the ship's doctor, Ellis, sat."

Carter mulled this over. "Any way you can check . . . ?"

She moved closer, excitement in her eyes. "I already

have. I got the ship's passenger list from the last cruise. Her name was Lenore Bonstedt then."

Carter sipped the brandy. She could have married Lundesburg in the meantime. That would account for the name change.

Then he remembered that first night at dinner, the overpowering musky perfume at the table. Juanita Gattling had been wearing it, but when she had left the table, the scent had remained, stronger than ever.

"If she was single then," Carter said, "could she have just been on the make for this Dr. Ellis?"

Sylvia chuckled. "Anything is possible, but I doubt it. The way she looks, and the way *he* looks, it would be like oil and water!"

"That bad?"

"Worse, Ellis is an overweight, supercilious ass. He fancies himself a ladies' man, but, believe me, even a fat, fifty, female hypochondriac would get turned off by his bedside manner."

"That puts a lot of pieces in the puzzle," Carter said, reaching for the phone.

"What are you going to do?"

"I feel ill, in need of the ship's doctor."

Sylvia shook her head. "No good, not until eight in the morning. His assistant is on call tonight. If you call the infirmary, you'll get him, not Ellis."

Carter replaced the phone and refilled his brandy glass. Then he told her about Juanita Gattling seeing a man emerge from his stateroom.

"Did she give you a description?"

"No, that will have to wait until morning as well. I checked. The tape was gone from the cassette. Also, it hasn't moved since I put another one in."

"They found the bug?"

Cater nodded. "So it would seem."

"Then it must be Schimmer."

"Maybe. Or Valanotti. Or both." Carter slammed the bar with his fist. "Dammit, even if we do away with the backup, I can't see any way to smoke Volga out."

Sylvia was at his side, running her hand up his arm. "Hey, we can't do anything until morning, and I'm not on call tonight . . ."

Carter turned, leaving his glass on the bar.

She had changed from the uniform into a figure-hugging dress that emphasized the swelling curves of her hips and breasts. Now she was staring at him with her enormous, gold-flecked eyes, sending all kinds of signals.

Suddenly he curved one arm under the back of her legs and lifted her. In ten long strides they were in the bedroom. He let her slide down his body until her heels found the floor.

She came to him, pushing the heavy cushions of her breasts hard against him. Her nails dug into the flesh beneath his shirt as her lips and tongue found his.

"Hey, you," he growled.

"Yes?"

"Get out of those damn clothes."

"Gladly."

He watched as the dress slithered to the floor. Her underwear was sheer, the bra accentuating her thrusting, pink-tipped breasts rather than hiding them. Through the sheer panties Carter could see the perfect triangle of hair.

The scantiness of the bra and panties added to the splendor of her long, tapering legs and the perfect curve of her flaring hips. Earlier, her long hair had been pulled back severely from her face and wide, curious eyes. Now it fell loosely, softening the features of her face and ending in a soft cascade down her back.

As she moved toward Carter it was with an athletic, animal grace that seemed to ripple the perfection of her body in all the most sensuous places.

And as she moved, the wispy pieces of nylon just disappeared. "Think I'm as sexy as Juanita Gattling?"

"Shut up," Carter chuckled, his hand slipping around behind her, caressing the silken smoothness of her back, the rounded curve of her naked buttocks.

He threw the rest of his clothes aside and pulled her to him. Her mouth was greedy under his, lips opening, tongue desperately seeking. He felt the marvelous texture of her skin against him as he forced her down onto the bed, and as his mouth sought her lush breasts, her thighs locked around him. She groaned deep in her throat.

"Nick." She made a sort of chant out of his name. "Nick, Nick, Nick, ahh, Nick . . ."

Her body rose to receive him, and the chant went on and on; and Carter forgot Volga and the combat ahead.

It was a combination of a change in the ship's movement and a different throb in the engines that awakened him.

He sat up in the bed, and it was a moment before he remembered that he wasn't alone. Sylvia was still asleep, her face beautiful in repose.

Carter slipped from the bed as gently as possible and moved to the glass doors that led to the narrow, railed balcony. Even as he parted them, he knew something was wrong. The big ship was moving in a wide circle, the fore and aft spotlights playing across the water. The engines were barely turning over, and there was scarcely any wake from the slow-moving bow.

"What is it?" Sylvia asked, sitting up and rubbing the sleep from her eyes.

"I don't know . . . yet," Carter replied, pulling on his clothes and moving to the door. "Stay here, I'll be right back."

The passageway was deserted. He moved out onto the promenade deck and walked aft until he spotted a steward hustling in his direction.

"What is it?" Carter asked. "What's going on?"

"We may have someone overboard. Excuse me, sir."

"Who is it?" The man ignored him and hurried on. Carter caught up and grasped his arm. "Who's overboard?"

"A woman, sir. A purse was found on the C-deck aft observation platform. One of the female passengers is missing."

Carter was suddenly cold. "Which female passenger?"

"Her name was Gattling, sir. Mrs. Harold Gattling."

FOURTEEN

Carter lounged on one of the upper sun decks and watched and waited. The ship had tied up nearly an hour earlier, but there had been no mad rush to get ashore.

Because of all the paperwork and legalities involved in the loss-at-sea of one of the passengers, the ship would be staying overnight in Tangier instead of having a sunset departure.

Harold Gattling had been the first one off the ship when it tied up. He had been escorted by the captain and two men who had arrived from the consulate.

The ship, of course, was a hotbed of rumor. Everyone had his or her idea as to just what had happened. Besides her purse, a pint bottle of gin had been found on the observation platform. There were two popular theories. The first was that Juanita had been drunk and simply fallen overboard. The second was that, in the middle of an arguement, Harold had beaned her and tossed her over.

The Killmaster had a third theory, and he was pretty sure it was valid.

From the first moment that night on the promenade deck when he had learned that there was a passenger overboard, and it was Juanita Gattling, his mind had made the connection.

It was a good bet that it was Lenore Lundesburg who had gone through Carter's stateroom that first day. Lenore had been near Carter by the pool when Juanita Gattling had told him about the man coming out of Carter's stateroom.

Carter didn't need many more facts to guess that the Lundesburg husband-and-wife team were KGB backups for Volga.

There was one more odd thread that Carter had tried, so far unsuccessfully, to weave into the puzzle. Why had Lenore—on the previous cruise, using the name Bonstedt —been so eager to sit at the dining table where the ship's doctor, Ellis, took his evening meals?

So far, Carter's attempts to get to Ellis had been futile. It seemed that the man was avoiding him in every way possible.

"You don't go ashore?"

Carter looked up. It was the German, Stavanger. "Perhaps later," Carter replied, reacting with the same distaste for the man that he had felt at their earlier meetings. Twice Carter had found himself sharing the same luncheon table with the man and he had hardly been able to eat. Stavanger stuffed his face like a desert nomad, as if every bite would be his last.

"I know Tangier well," the man said. "The old city, the better rug and gem merchants. I also know the finest whorehouses. Perhaps you would like to join me?"

"No, thanks," Carter replied. "If I do go ashore, it will probably be for just a quick lunch."

The man merely nodded, lighting a small cigar, his interest on the gangway and the exiting passengers. It was several moments before he spoke again.

"A terrible accident, that woman falling overboard."

"Yes, it was."

"You knew her, I think?"

"We had the same table at dinner." Carter was trying to think of a logical excuse to get away from the man.

Suddenly Stavanger leaned over and played locker-room confidant. "I've heard she tried to sleep with every man on the ship. Were you so lucky?"

"No, I wasn't," Carter said, putting a bite into his words.

"Me neither. It was probably the husband. He caught her playing around, and, poof! Well, I must go."

Carter didn't reply, and Stavanger ambled off. He killed another fifteen minutes, and then headed for the infirmary to make another try at a private talk with Ellis.

"Yes, may I help you?"

"I seem to have acquired a queasy stomach. I wonder if I could see Dr. Ellis?"

"Dr. Ellis has gone ashore. I am his assistant, Dr. Reisling. What are the symptoms?"

Carter gave the man enough symptoms to equal diptheria and malaria, and the doctor unlocked a chest of bottles.

Dr. Reisling, Carter thought, wouldn't inspire a lot of confidence. Besides his practically unintelligible accent, the man looked like an abortionist in the bad old days of kitchen-table surgery. Without the white doctor's coat smeared with cigarette ash and minus the stethoscope around his neck, he might have been the operator of a Hamburg tattoo parlor.

"Take two of these after every meal for the next couple of days. That should take care of it."

"Thank you."

The man merely nodded and turned away, lighting a fresh cigarette from the butt between his lips.

Carter started to leave, and paused at the door. "Excuse me . . ."

"Yes?"

"Isn't is odd to have two doctors on the staff, and no nurse?"

The minute he said it, the Killmaster wished he had only thought it. The man's eyes suddenly came alive, burning into Carter's. He could almost see the wheels turning, coming up with a reasonable answer.

"Not necessarily. Each of us must take several cruises as training before we can become head of staff ourselves."

"Of course." Carter held up the bottle of pills. "Thanks again."

Five minutes after Carter had returned to his cabin to change to go ashore, Horst Stavanger slipped into the infirmary.

"Well?"

"The same. He wanted to see Ellis. I'd say he suspects something but knows nothing for sure . . . yet."

"Then," Stavanger said, "I might not wait for the reply from Moscow on the photo."

"Evor?"

Stavanger nodded. "His bloodlust should be well satisfied before this job is over."

It was nearly five when Carter left the ship at last. He took a cab from the pier area to the center of the new city and then strolled. He spent nearly two hours moving in and out of the tiny shops. When he was sure he wasn't being followed, he jumped into a taxi.

"Do you know Leduc's, on the Rabat road?"

The driver made a face, nodded, and the cab jerked away from the curb. It was a twenty-minute ride, and Carter checked the rear all the way. If a tail had managed to stay with him, Carter couldn't detect him.

He got out of the cab and leaned back in through the passenger-side window. The young driver's eyes became saucers when he saw the thick pile of bills in Carter's hand. They grew even wider when the bills, one by one, started floating to the seat beside him.

"This should take care of the fare. I want you to come back for me at midnight. But first, I want a very large favor."

"Monsieur has just purchased me and the cab for a week."

Carter smiled. "One night will do. I want you to go right to where you picked me up . . ."

"I would do that anyway, monsieur. The roundabout on the Boulevard Mohammed V is the only place to pick up foreigners."

"I know that," Carter replied, letting the pile of bills mount, "but there is more. A man, perhaps a man and a woman, will get into your cab. They will probably tell you they are friends of mine. They will ask you where you have taken me . . ."

Now the glad expression on the driver's face was changing, the wide smile disappearing and the eyes narrowing. "Monsieur is not a dope runner. I have no wish to—"

"No dope. Don't worry, *mon ami,* the rest is simple. All you have to do is come back and describe the people to me, exactly what they look like."

The driver's shrugged and patted the money. "As you wish, monsieur. It is as good as done. Uh, one more thing . . ."

"Yes?"

"When they ask me where I took you, what do I tell them?"

Carter smiled and dropped a last bill. "Why, you tell them the truth, of course."

He waited until the cab had rounded the corner and then he entered Pierre Leduc's.

It was a basement affair with a couple of slot machines to the left of the door and the bar itself along the wall to the right. There were a couple of tables and a jukebox that had to be pre-World War II at the rear of the room. Carter knew that the only music on the box was mournful ditties by Parisian chanteuses and a dozen different versions of the Marseillaise.

The stools in front of the bar were old, with peeling vinyl covers. Nearly all of them were occupied by the roughest bunch of characters in North Africa. Leduc's had a reputation to uphold: If you didn't like to drink and fight, don't drop in.

Carter picked one of the tables away from the bar where he could watch both the front door and the passageway from the rear door.

"Oui, monsieur?"

She was about sixteen, with black hair piled in a glossy heap high on her head. Her features were as clean-cut as those of a cameo, with enormous black eyes, and her breasts stood high and firm without support. In about five years she would be rollickingly fat, but right now she was at the peak of perfection, like ripened fruit.

"Whiskey, in the bottle. And tell the man that the bottle is for the American."

"Oui, monsieur." Her hips played a tune all her own as she moved away.

No one had even glanced at Carter when he entered. All of the attention was riveted in the other direction, where two gorilla types with domed heads and flat faces were having a drunken argument with the man, Pierre Leduc.

Leduc was a tall stringbean of a man, with sleeves rolled above big wristbones. He pointed a long, bony finger at the two men and said something in a voice pitched low so it didn't carry.

One of the men replied in a voice that did. "I think *monsieur le patron* is the son of a whore! I have cut the balls off better men than he in the Congo!"

Carter smiled, lit a cigarette, and sat back to wait for the fun to start.

It didn't take long.

It was as if the tall Frenchman had leaped from a springboard. He jackknifed his legs, and in one smooth leap was standing on the bar.

A long, ugly knife appeared in one of the men's hands.

Leduc's right foot lashed out and the knife spun across the room, the left following in a blur, its toe colliding with the man's mouth.

He screamed, spitting teeth and blood, and windmilled back, upsetting the stool. He kept going, falling across one of the tables, flattening it.

Number Two lurched toward Leduc, managing to wrap his beefy arms around the rangy Frenchman's legs. Leduc merely dropped to his knees and chopped each side of the man's neck.

Carter could hear at least one collarbone pop, and saw the man stagger back, his throat screaming out his pain.

The man with the ruptured mouth was back on his feet. Like a cat, Leduc dropped from the bar to the floor. They came together, but it was no match. Leduc curled his fingers around the backs of their necks. The wiry arms came together and Carter heard the crack of skull against skull.

Both men dropped without further sound or struggle.

"Pierre!"

It was the girl. The third member of the trio had retrieved Number One's knife. Slowly he was approaching Leduc with the knife in both hands. Even though he had the weapon, it was obvious from the way his hands shook who had the upper hand.

"The knife, monsieur, put it on the bar," Leduc said, his voice a raspy whisper. "Put it on the bar now or I will take it away from you and slice you from breastbone to crotch."

The man stopped, sweat dripping into his eyes from a shiny forehead. Then he tossed the knife onto the bar with a muttered oath.

Leduc himself uttered an oath and caught the man's arm, twisted it and locked it behind him.

He marched the man the length of the bar, stopped a few feet from the door, took careful aim, and used his foot.

There was a shout of pain and the man seemed to soar. He crashed against the door, went through, and spilled face-down onto the sidewalk.

Leduc grabbed the unconscious pair on the floor by the back of their belts and dragged them to the door. He tossed them out, then turned to look at the other men at the bar who still leaned over their drinks.

"Anyone else?" His voice was a whisper, but it carried and there was a smile on his face.

As if by magic, the bar was just as it had been when Carter entered. The music came back up from the jukebox, the chatter started again, and the girl moved through the tables.

Carter smiled to himself. Just another night at Leduc's, he thought.

Leduc swung behind the bar, grabbed a bottle and two glasses, and, with a wide grin on his angular face, headed toward Carter's table.

"*Bonsoir, mon ami*. Sorry about the service."

Carter shrugged. "Business first."

Leduc poured and raised his glass. "To God and the American dollar."

"To life," Carter said, and they both drank. "What do you have for me?"

"Evidently not much more than when you sailed. The Italian woman, Valanotti, has a child. Your people seem to think it could be the German's, Schimmer."

"Their affair at the university?"

Leduc nodded. "Also an interesting tidbit on the wife of Schimmer."

"The one in East Germany, in a mental hospital?"

"*Oui*. It seems she is not in a mental hospital. She was a plant from the day of their marriage. She tried to turn Schimmer, and he wouldn't go for it. They threatened blackmail, and Schimmer went right to the West German government. The Eastern side pulled her before she was arrested. The West Germans fabricated the story about her being crazy and the mental hospital in East Germany so that the scandal wouldn't affect Schimmer's work."

Carter sipped the second glass of whiskey and mulled this over. It could be a double twist to make Schimmer more solid, but he didn't think so. Too much trouble to achieve the same end. "What about the others?"

"Clean, nothing to even suspect them."

"There is less light at the end of this tunnel every day," Carter growled in disgust. "What about Dalton's secretary, Monica Sims? She sits in on all the meetings."

Leduc squinted his eyes in concentration. Carter waited. He was familiar with the way the Frenchman worked. He had a tremendous capacity for memorization. He rarely wrote anything down. In the past, it had saved his skin several times.

"They rechecked her background and she came out clean. Besides the obvious, being Dalton's part-time mistress, she is invaluable in many ways. She is an accomplished mathematician and has an aptitude for collating massive amount of figures. A lot of people think Dalton's success in the last three years came from Sims's ability to apply what he dreams up. They rechecked and she's as clean as the five principals."

Carter put his fingers to his temples and rubbed.

Could Volga be a bystander, someone outside the circle? Impossible.

Volga would have to have access to the material. To do that, Volga would have to be in on all the correspondence and the current meetings.

"Pierre . . ."

Carter opened his eyes. It was the young girl.

"Oui?"

"It is Hasak. He wishes to settle his bill."

"It is about time," Leduc said.

"He says the figure is four-seventy-two."

"He is wrong."

Carter listened as Leduc rattled off a day-by-day account of the man's drinking bill and gambling losses. The girl wrote each figure down as he spoke, nodded when he finished, and moved away.

"It's amazing how you do that."

Leduc shrugged. "It is part gift, part training. As a boy in Algiers, keeping all records in one's head was a way to defeat the tax man."

Slowly a wave of realization came over Carter. "Leduc, just how much can you remember?"

"Anything I wish," the Frenchman said, and shrugged. "It is a matter of total concentration."

"Even if it wasn't written down in the first place, if it was only spoken?"

"Of course."

Suddenly Carter knew how Volga operated.

Now it was a question of how to make sure he knew the identity of Volga.

FIFTEEN

The jukebox was turned down low. All the lights had been turned off except two dim bulbs behind the bar. It was almost one in the morning and the customers had long since been dispersed by Leduc. The Frenchman himself was somewhere out in the night.

Carter sat with the girl at a table in the center of the room, a bottle between them.

The taxi driver had returned at five minutes before midnight. What he had told Carter after slipping in through the rear door had been illuminating.

"There were two men, monsieur, not a man and a woman."

Carter had listened gravely to the driver's description of the two men, then sent him on his way. Then he had huddled with Leduc.

"They won't use guns," Carter had said, "only as a last resort. And neither will I. If possible, I want to take one of them alive."

"Then use this," Leduc said, passing Carter the knife he had taken earlier in the bar fight.

Now they sat, waiting.

"They are not coming," the girl whispered, keeping up the pretense by running her hand up Carter's leg under the table.

"They'll come," Carter said, sliding one finger across her ample breast and kissing her lightly on the lips.

All at once the girl's eyes flickered away from him,

147

over his shoulder, toward the hallway leading into the bar from the rear door. "He is here, the tall blond one."

Carter turned in his chair. "Lundesburg, what are you doing so far from the city?"

The man's eyes checked the room, under every table and behind the bar. When he was satisfied that there were just the three of them, he spoke. "I was drinking at another bar down the street. They told me there that I could find a good woman here. I saw you through the front window."

Carter laughed. "Sorry, old man, you're out of luck. I'm afraid the only woman in this place is mine for the night. But let me buy you a drink."

He nodded his head toward the bar. The girl stood. As she passed the big Swede, he grabbed her arm. In the same motion, he twisted her into him and put a knife to her throat.

"I'm not thirsty." He was calm, the eyes steady, not a quiver in the hand holding the knife. "Stand up and turn around Carter."

"Carter? My name is—"

"Your name is Nick Carter. We sent a photograph to Moscow and got a reply at the consulate tonight. Sit there and don't move."

He shoved the girl into a chair, spun Carter around, and bent him over a table. With the blade at the back of Carter's neck, he skillfully ran his free hand all over the Killmaster's body.

"You're a brave man to travel the underbelly of Tangier without a weapon."

"Why would I need a weapon?" Carter said lightly.

The blow was sharp, across his shoulder. It was meant to be painful, not disabling. Carter took it and maintained his position.

"Who else do you have on the ship?" the Swede hissed.

Carter decided to get to the point and do away with any further pretense. "I'll give you a chance to run, Lundesburg. Just give me Volga's identity."

The big Swede cursed and hit Carter again. The Killmaster rolled with this punch and hit the floor practically at the girl's feet.

"I could offer you the same thing in return for information," the Swede replied. "But you've just told me what I want to know."

Carter's eyes met the girl's. He nodded. Her hands grasped her skirt and pulled it to her waist. The long-bladed knife was along her inner thigh, held there by a garter.

Carter grasped the knife with one hand and shoved her chair back with the other. He didn't even try to withdraw the knife. He simply turned it, slitting the garter at the same time he rolled.

The Swede's knife thudded into the wooden floor inches from Carter's shoulder.

The girl hit the floor and rolled, putting distance between herself and the two men.

Behind him, Carter heard the Swede curse and the sound of the knife being withdrawn. Then he was on his feet and turning.

Lundesburg was in a crouch, the knife up and ready. "You knew."

Carter nodded, giving the man an insolent grin. "I knew. I'm not going to kill you outright, Evor. I'm going to skin you, peel you until you start talking."

"You are a fool."

It began.

The Swede feinted, well, and his blade drove for Carter's gut. The Killmaster had already hooked a chair with his toe. He caught it with his free hand and jammed the back into the other man. It came up hard and high, catching Lundesburg under the chin, knocking him off-balance.

"Who is Volga, Lundesburg?"

"Believe it or not, Carter, I don't know. Not that it matters . . ."

Then he was circling. Carter was moving with him, the two of them like poised panthers between the tables, each sizing up the other's stance and balance, strengths and weaknesses.

Then the Swede, with a snakelike hissing sound between his teeth, moved.

His hand was quick, darting like a striking viper. Carter caught the blade on his own, turning it aside and parrying. Lundesburg dodged, his body as agile as a bullfighter's, and the thrust was wide.

But it was almost the first score, and Carter saw beads of sweat pop out on the other man's face. And he saw something else: grudging respect in the other man's eyes.

The tall blond came again, this time in earnest, wanting it over with quickly. The blade arched at Carter's throat, then changed direction and plunged for his belly. The Killmaster stepped back nimbly and the slashing edge only got a portion of his shirt.

"Close, but no cigar, Lundesburg."

The frustrated Swede tried a backhand. Carter went under it with his blade up, and cut a ten-inch slash in the man's arm. The Swede roared, more in anger than pain, and recovered with another straightforward jab. This one caught another piece of Carter's shirt, but failed to find flesh.

The Swede finished the thrust off-balance. The Killmaster countered with doubled-armed slashes, shifting the blade from hand to hand each time. The result was one very bloody chest.

Lundesburg stepped back and looked down at himself in amazement.

"I told you," Carter growled, "I don't need to kill you. Let's talk."

The man looked up with pure hatred in his eyes. When the fresh attack came it wasn't at Carter; it was directed at the girl. The knife came up like lightning from the floor. If it would have struck, she would have been gutted like a fish.

But it didn't.

Again, Carter locked blades and got a grip on the other man's neck with his free hand. Their faces were close, so close that Carter could smell the other man's dinner on his breath.

And their eyes locked.

It was then that Carter knew it was useless. The man knew only one thing, kill or be killed. Compromise was not programmed into his brain.

Carter intentionally gave ground. The Swede's blade slipped loose and thrust at Carter's chest. The Killmaster twisted so it went between arm and body.

He felt the whisper of it as, once more, it slashed fabric. Then he wrenched his left hand away from Lundesburg's grappling left and with a smooth shifting motion threw the knife from right to left. His right went out and caught the Swede's knife hand, even as his left came over wielding the blade.

The change in hands, the change in balance, caught Lundesburg totally unprepared. Carter slit, quickly, expertly, and Lundesburg screamed. The knife dropped from his hand and blood poured down his chest from his severed throat.

He clawed at himself and gasped for air, air that had no conduit to his lungs.

Carter stepped back, kicking the other man's knife across the room.

Lundesburg's eyes rolled up into his skull, came down again, and found Carter's. He was dying, his blood spurting through splayed fingers. He knew it, and the realization threw him into a panic.

He crashed over a few tables, his hands trying to stem the tide, and finally he sank to his knees. He stared at Carter for a long moment with eyes that were no longer fierce, only horrified.

Then he made an inarticulate gurgling sound in his throat and, wheeling, blood still spurting, he fell on his face.

The girl, calm through it all, stepped forward and leaned over him. Daintily, she pressed two fingers to the side of his throat and then rolled her eyes up at Carter.

"Mort, monsieur."

"Can you handle it?"

"Of course."

"Then do it. There's another one out there somewhere."

She nodded and Carter headed for the back door.

In the shafts of moonlight coming through holes into the decaying muslin awnings stretched between the buildings, the narrow, cobbled alley looked like a sewer. By day it was a marketplace. Now it was a perfect spot to be either hunted or hunter. Carter was both.

He moved to his right, into the darkness toward the center of the tented area. Garbage was strewn across the cobbles, and the dogs fighting each other to eat it did it silently.

After the beer-and-sweat perfume of the bar, the alley-like street held a stench that jolted Carter's stomach. It was the stench of general rot from the crumbling plaster walls, of human and animal excrement, of halves of sheep carcasses dangling from iron hooks in the open with swarms of angry flies covering them.

And somewhere out there in the darkness was the German, Stavanger. Carter had already cursed himself for not guessing. Had he interpreted better on the ship, all this might not have been necessary.

But it was too late to think about that now. Now he must bait the German.

There was a sound in a darkened doorway. Carter flattened against the wall, not breathing, and narrowed his eyes.

An old man in a ragged djellaba sat puffing on a red-hosed water pipe and staring back at Carter from vacant eyes.

The Killmaster moved on to the mouth of the alley and turned right. In no time he had reached the mud street that ran in front of Leduc's.

Reaching the street, he stopped and checked it out. In yet another alley directly across from the bar he saw faint movement.

He smiled.

Would Stavanger come to his comrade's aid when the time went on? Or would he leave him and go back to the ship to regroup?

Carter figured the latter, and retraced his steps. At the other end of the alley he climbed and went over rooftops until he was some distance below the bar. Then he darted across the street and came back up.

Just short of the alley, he climbed again and padded softly over the rooftops. At the edge above the alley, he stopped abruptly and dropped into a low crouch.

Stavanger was right below him, intent on the darkened

windows and the door of the bar. Carter could see the dark glint of a silenced automatic in the man's hand at his side.

Carter came off the roof like a shadow. His weight drove the other man to the ground. Carter's fingers curled around his mouth, jerking his head back. The butt of the Killmaster's knife slammed the knuckles of the German's right fist, dislodging the automatic. Carter kicked it out of reach with his knee.

He guessed that Lundesburg was the muscle, the assassin, and Stavanger was the liaison. That meant little chance of him talking, but Carter had to try.

"The Swede is dead."

A grunt.

"If you want to die, Stavanger, I can accommodate you. If not, I want answers."

The German twisted his entire body savagely, using all his enormous strength to buck the weight off him. The instant he threw Carter off, or thought he did, he was scrambling after the gun.

His fingers were closing around it when the heel of a shoe came down hard against the back of his neck, exactly at the base of his skull, with all of Carter's weight behind it.

Stavanger heard, as though from a long way off, the splintering of spinal bones as his neck broke.

For a long moment Carter remained standing over the body, spread-legged, his breath rasping harshly through his teeth. Finally, the tension inside him let go a little. He picked up the gun. It was Russian, probably obtained at the consulate.

He stuck it in the pocket of his jacket and bent to the body. He transferred everything he found in Stavanger's pockets to the same pockets of his own clothing. A polaroid photograph of himself and a printout announcing his real identity, he burned, grinding the ashes into the mud under his heel.

Then he checked the street, darted across and into the bar.

The girl stood in the center of the room. Nearby were two blank-faced men in dark djellabas. There was no sign of Evor Lundesburg. Even the bloodstains had been scrubbed from the floor.

"The other one is across the street in the alley."

She nodded, said a few terse words in Arabic to the two men, and they darted out the door.

"Here are his things."

Carter took Lundesburg's watch, ring, wallet, and stateroom key from her, adding them to Stavanger's in his pockets.

"Did Pierre call?"

She nodded. "He has many eyes. Several pair of them spotted your doctor and followed him from the ship."

"And?"

"He spent the evening in a whorehouse in the Moine section near the airport."

"And now?"

"He goes into the hills toward the Rif, to a place where they make the dope."

Carter smiled and almost sighed with relief. It had only been a guess, but now it looked as if rich ore had been found.

"I'll need a car," he said.

"I will drive you."

SIXTEEN

Simon Deveraux was bone-tired, but the job was done and the result was ready for the mule, Ellis.

He removed his rubber apron with fingers trembling with weariness. On a tray before him were six clear plastic bags, kilos of heroin. It was high quality. But then it always was.

He was a short, thick-chested man with a pointy beard. He was fifty-seven, and right now he looked and felt much older. His eyes were bloodshot and the flesh under them was puffy and dark. He had a splitting headache from inhaling too many of the fumes from the acetic and hydrochloric acids he'd use in the process of transforming the base morphine into pure heroin.

Outside the mud-brick farmhouse, he heard a car. Almost at once the door opened and one of the guards poked his head in.

"He comes."

"The signal?" Deveraux asked.

"As always," the head said nodding.

"The bags are there."

The guard entered, slinging his rifle over his shoulder, and began to gather the bags.

Outside, Deveraux sucked his lungs full of the cool night air. He could see the rented Citroën bouncing over the ruts in the narrow lane, approaching slowly. He dug some aspirin from his pocket and walked to the well near the house. Another guard slouched there, his rifle across his chest, his eyes also on the car.

"He's late."

Deveraux nodded, swallowing the aspirin. "The whores probably took longer than usual. It's just as well. I just finished."

The car came to a halt in the muddy yard and Deveraux crossed to it. Ellis got out, looking his usual sweaty, nervous self.

"*Bonsoir,* Monsieur Ellis. A good crossing this time?"

"Yes, yes, as usual. Is it ready?"

"Of course."

Ellis reached into the car and came out with his medical bag. He set it on the hood and ran a trembling finger along its bottom until there was a click. The side opened in the bag to reveal a false bottom.

"After all these times you still sweat, Ellis?"

"I can't help it."

Carefully, he shoved the bags into the bottom of the bag, distributing them evenly, and closed the valise.

Deveraux took a form from his pocket not unlike any form that could be found in a warehouse dealing in pharmaceuticals. Printed on it was a list of medicines.

Ellis scrawled his name across the bottom of it and climbed back into the car.

"*Au revoir, monsieur,*" Deveraux said. "Next month, same time, same place."

Oh, no, Ellis thought, turning the car around and bouncing down the lane. *No more, this is the last time!*

At the main road, he turned back toward Tangier and stomped on the accelerator. It took him exactly twenty-five minutes to drive back to the suburb of Moine. He parked the car in front of the rental agency and walked toward the all-night café two blocks away.

There was always a taxi at the café. In all the times he had made pickups, he had never failed to get one no matter the time of night.

He was halfway there, at the mouth of a narrow side street, when a voice came to him from the darkness.

"Monsieur?"

She stepped into the illumination of a streetlight several doors up. She was young, very young, and quite beautiful. She was the kind of girl Ellis had always asked them for but never got.

"Is monsieur lonely tonight?" she purred. Then she pulled her blouse open. She wore nothing beneath it. Her breasts were lush, the same olive color as her face, and they were big of nipple, their points standing out hard and erect. She put her hands under them in a seductive gesture, and lifted them as if offering them to him.

"No ... I ..."

"Come here, monsieur, for just a moment."

Ellis was drawn to her like a magnet. She ran her hands over her breasts, luring him. Then she ran her hands down her body and parted her skirt. There was nothing under that, either.

"Perhaps if you give me your name, a telephone number ... the next time ..."

"Closer, monsieur. In the darkness so no one can see us."

Her hand pulled his head down. Her lips opened wide with a great hunger. She was rubbing herself against him.

Then he felt it, sharp, pressing into his swollen belly.

"Wha ..."

"It is a knife, monsieur. There is a car behind me. I

want you to keep walking toward it, quietly. If you don't I will decorate this filthy street with your manhood . . . what there is of it."

"Is that all of it?"

"It is, all I know, I swear!"

Dr. Everett Ellis was a mess. He had wet himself and now he was a shambles of fear, with his arms wrapped around his body as though he were freezing even though it was at least ninety degrees in the little room.

"And you're sure about the drugs he'll use?"

"Yes," Ellis whimpered, "positive. I looked in the case he brought aboard. He keeps it in my safe in the infirmary."

"Give it to me again, the sequence."

"Whoever the person is, they will take Peradraxin. In small amounts it is not dangerous, but it brings on a heavy fever and a near comatose state."

"Then this Reisling delivers another drug . . ."

"Yes, Monopraxaline. It's illegal, not sold on any market in the States."

"How do you know about it, Ellis?"

More tears ran down his face and he hugged himself harder. "I've smuggled it into the States."

"You're just a regular little runner, aren't you? What happens then?"

He blubbered, but finally managed to speak. "The interaction of the two drugs brings on a catatonic state. So much so that the individual appears dead. There is no neurological response, no perceptible vital signs. Only a physician could determine the difference."

"Then what happens?"

"I sign the death certificate as the examining physician."

Carter only nodded. So that's how Volga would get off the ship.

He almost had it all now. There were only a couple of little points to add, and he was fairly sure he knew where he could get those. Ellis broke back into his thoughts.

"W-what are you going to do with me?"

"For the time being, nothing. If you're a good boy, maybe nothing in the future."

"If I don't deliver in Miami, they'll kill me."

"That's right," Carter said. "Absolutely right, and I've got the dope. If you want it back to deliver, you'll do exactly as I tell you. What do you say?"

"What choice do I have?"

"None. When you get back to the ship, I want you to tell Reisling that the dope run took longer than you expected. Give him a list of drugs you need for stock and send him ashore."

"What if he won't go?"

"It's up to you to make him go. Because if he doesn't, Ellis, I'll kill him and put him in your freezer."

"God, oh God . . ."

"He's not likely to help you either. There's a shower in there. Get yourself cleaned up."

Without another word, Carter left the room. Leduc and the girl were waiting.

"Give me about a half hour. Make sure he's cleaned up, then drop him off at the ship."

Leduc snorted. "You think, monsieur, that this piece of crap can pull this off?"

"He's the best I've got," Carter admitted. "Just make sure this Reisling doesn't get back to the ship."

He headed for the door, but Leduc's voice stopped him.

"What about the bags . . . the dope?"

Carter mused for a moment, then smiled. "Scatter it in the bay. Let the fish get a good high."

Carter eased the key into the lock and turned it gently. There was a faint click and he turned the knob. Carefully, he pushed the door open, slid inside, and closed it behind him.

In sleep, with her mouth slightly slack, her hair in disarray, and without makeup, she wasn't so beautiful.

One of the glass doors leading to the narrow balcony was open. A soft breeze rustled the drapes slightly, letting the first rays of dawn peek through.

On soundless feet he padded toward the bed. Halfway there, she seemed to sense his presence.

"Evor . . . is it done?" One eye came open, then two, and she was bolting from the bed.

Carter caught one shoulder. The thin material of her nightgown ripped and it parted to the waist. She slipped away and clawed at the drawer of a nightstand.

Carter didn't hesitate. He curled his fingers in her thick hair and yanked her backward. At the same time, he flung her toward the bed. The back of her head made a dull thud against the headboard.

He yanked the drawer open. A Beretta automatic gleamed up at him from its perch on a layer of scarves.

She came for him again, her naked breasts dancing, fear and hatred in her eyes, her long fingernails clawing the air. He managed to get his hand in her face and shove, hard. She rolled like a ball over the bed and Carter moved to the drapes.

He opened them, stepped out onto the balcony, and took a look at the terraces to the right and left. They were empty. He tossed the Beretta into the sea and stepped back into the room.

She was slightly more docile now, more fear than hate in her eyes, as she tried to pull the nightgown back together and cover her nakedness.

"Who do you think you are! How dare you—"

"Shut up." He picked up a satin robe from the foot of the bed and tossed it to her.

She shrugged into the robe. Suddenly she was surprisingly calm. "My husband will be back . . ."

"No, he won't," Carter said, his voice tight. "*If* he is your husband, you're a widow."

"Evor? You're lying!"

Carter tossed the wallet, the watch, and the ring onto the bed between them, and followed it with the key.

The change was instant. She went from pink to white and looked a little sick.

Then he pulled the second half of a double whammy. He took the German's possessions from his pockets and dropped them on the bed next to the others. "And Stavanger is fish food as well."

It was the last blow. She sat on the other twin bed and hugged the robe around her. If he hadn't known it before, he knew it now. Of the three, this woman was the weak link. He decided to go with all the marbles and hit her hard enough to remove her last crutch.

"Where's your pill?"

"What?"

"What, hell! You've got a cyanide pill for emergencies like this. Where is it?"

She stared at him for a long moment, then her slender shoulders sagged. "Shoe," she mumbled. "Green satin slippers . . . heel."

The Killmaster yanked open the closet doors and found a cloth shoe rack attached to one wall. Out of the twenty or so pairs, there was only one pair of green satin slippers. He tapped one heel against the other. The heel of the right was hollow.

He broke it off. The inside of the hollowed-out heel was cloth. He turned it over and a hard gelatin capsule dropped into his hand.

At the minibar he poured a glass of water from a partially full pitcher, then he moved between the beds.

Her eyes hadn't followed him. She sat staring, as if in disbelief, at what was left of her two comrades on the opposite bed.

Carter put the glass of water in her right hand and pried open the fingers in her left. When he dropped the pill into her palm, she reacted much as he had hoped she would. She let out a little squeak of fear and looked up at him with haunted eyes.

"What are you doing?"

"Giving you a choice," he replied. "Take the pill, kill yourself, as you've been instructed to do. Or do as I say."

Now he saw an emotion other than fear on her face and in her eyes. Her lips curled and she almost spat at him. "You don't give a damn, do you!"

"Not in the least. Take your choice."

She looked down at the ice-blue gelatin capsule, up at Carter, and then down again.

Her shoulders shook and a low wail came out of her mouth. He smoked, leaning casually against a nearby bureau. Slowly she brought herself back.

"It means defection. What can you guarantee me?"

"No deals."

"But I'll need a new identity, cover, money."

"No deals. I'll see what I can do." He looked at his watch. "Make up your mind. I've got a busy morning."

"You son of a bitch!"

"Agreed . . . I am. Well?"

She threw the capsule and the glass of water across the room. Carter crushed out his cigarette and sat on the opposite bed, facing her.

"Good. Now the big question first. Who is Volga?"

"I don't know."

"That's what Lundesburg said."

"It's the truth. Can I have a cigarette?" He opened his case and lit it for her. She puffed quickly, without inhaling, à la Bette Davis. "None of us knew. It was part of security. Our only job was backup, to take you people out."

"Who ID'd me?"

"A Mexican doctor. Evidently he treated your wounds when you were running with Prokudin."

"Figures. What about vice versa? Does Volga know you?"

"I don't think so. Stavanger, maybe. He was liaison to Rome."

"Rome?"

She nodded, killing the cigarette. "A KGB colonel in Rome. He is control on High Dive. Everything comes from him, in case there's an emergency."

"So there is an alternate?" Carter asked.

"Yes. If there's a leak, or if we couldn't stop you, Volga will disembark early, probably in Istanbul."

"Okay, we'll get back to that. Tell me about Dr. Ellis."

She rattled it off. It was rolling out of her now and Carter could tell that she wasn't holding anything back. As she talked, he started pacing.

"After he signed the death certificate and accompanied the body ashore, he would be disposed of when the ship reached Athens."

"Lundesburg?"

She nodded. "An accident."

Carter went to the windows. He took several minutes to

put it together before he turned back to face her. "In case anything happened to Stavanger, were you and Lundesburg given the Rome contact?"

"Yes, we both were told the cover address. It's a woman, I think the colonel's mistress. The code book is an American novel, *God's Little Acre*. The key is in the lining of Stavanger's briefcase."

"So, if necessary, you could send the alert?"

"Yes."

Now he was standing directly in front of her, his voice as cold as his eyes. "We have seven more days of sailing until we reach Istanbul. Tonight, at dinner, you will inform the dining room steward and those at the table that your husband was called away on business. Understand?"

"Yes."

"Then tomorrow you will become ill, a touch of sea-sickness. From tomorrow on, you will not leave your cabin until I tell you to. Do you understand that?"

"And if I don't?"

"Then we'll have another passenger overboard at sea."

Leaving her with that, Carter left the stateroom and went topside. On the forward part of the sky deck, he ordered coffee and waited. Twenty minutes later he saw Dr. Reisling scurry down the gangway.

There was a cab waiting.

Even from such a great distance, Carter could recognize the driver. Pierre Leduc.

He went into the sky deck restaurant and ordered breakfast. By the time he had finished, the ship was again at sea.

SEVENTEEN

For the next three days, Carter kept tabs on all five of the scientists and Monica Sims. Outwardly, the sudden absence of Evor Lundesburg and Stavanger didn't seem to affect any of them.

From Roy Hooper, Carter had gotten a key to Stavanger's stateroom and obtained the paperback novel of Erskine Caldwell's *God's Little Acre*, and the page key from the briefcase.

Sylvia kept him informed on the meetings. Evidently a great deal of progress had been made. The meetings had been cut down from a full eight hours to three in the mornings.

"And when they come out of there now, there are smiles on all their faces."

"Yeah," Carter had replied, "those smiles won't last long after they leave the ship."

Lenore Lundesburg, aka Bonstedt, was following orders. She seemed resigned now, and had even reverted to inviting Carter to share her bed, in hopes that sex would help her personal cause when the mess was over.

It had taken a couple of late-night nudging talks to keep the ship's doctor in line and calm, but it had worked.

Two days out of Istanbul, Carter had Sylvia set up a brief meeting with the first officer. Carter lied his ears off, but the man finally agreed to allow a brief conference with the captain. Carter pleaded a pressing personal problem that only the captain could resolve

"Come in!"

Carter entered. One half of the captain's personal stateroom also served as an office.

"Mr. Stevens?"

"Captain Walters."

He was tall, slender, and dressed in a uniform with knife-sharp creases. His handshake, like the scowl on his face, was hard and dry.

"I hope this won't take too long. I've a great deal to do."

Carter gauged this salty English sea captain. He was about fifty-five, with close-cut, silver hair, a lean brown face, a straight no-nonsense nose, a square jaw, a stubborn chin, all of which somehow became diffused and softened because of the great big clear, somehow sad, compassionate gray eyes. It was a face that gave off many intricate facets, and made Carter decide to come right to the point.

"First of all, Captain, my name isn't Stevens. It's Carter and I am an agent of the United States government." He spread his credentials out on the desk in front of the captain.

The head bowed slightly and two fingers rubbed his temples. "Why me . . . and my ship, whatever the hell it is?"

"I'm sorry, sir, but I didn't choose the *Grecian Mist*."

"All right, what is it?"

"I don't expect you to grant me any request without some authorization. May I borrow your pad?"

Reluctantly, the captain slid a memo pad across the desk. Carter spoke as he wrote.

"Washington has already notified your MI6 of my mission. I want you to send this telex to a man named Giles Henderson. The telex code is already known. I'm also asking that you use your oldest and most reliable communications man, one who is above reproach. This telex, and the return, is for your eyes only."

He tore the page off the pad and passed it over. The captain read it, scowled harder, and stood.

"Excuse me."

"Of course."

He left, and Carter lit a cigarette. The captain was back in ten minutes.

"It will take about an hour. Something to drink?"

"No, thank you."

"Too early?"

"No, not really," Carter replied with a slight grin. "There's just too much to do first."

"Something to eat, then? Breakfast?"

"Thank you," Carter said, and knew that Captain Walters would give him every assistance possible.

He was hungry. He ordered three eggs lightly scrambled with sausage patties well-done, buttered toast, and coffee. It seemed the captain was also hungry. He ordered a ham steak with hash brown potatoes and a single poached egg, buttered toast, and coffee.

Until the food came, they sparred, still like fighters in the early rounds in a prize ring, jabbing away with inconsequential small talk. When the food arrived, they ate but continued to feel each other out, jabbing away with the small talk. Then, with the plates cleared and new pots of coffee, and Carter with a cigarette and the captain with a thin aromatic cigar, the reply came from London. Captain Walters read it and looked up. He was smiling.

"It seems you have powerful friends, Mr. Carter. Anything short of the ship itself is yours."

Carter smiled. "I'll need far less than the ship, sir. Actually, just a few of its services, and, when the time comes, no questions asked by you or your crew."

True to his word, the captain agreed to everything Carter had planned, as well as swearing himself to silence. The Killmaster didn't tell him everything, of course, only what he would need to know to satisfy the plan.

Carter returned to his stateroom and sat down to compose the telex to Rome.

The key pages for this date were 140 through 146. He went through the words from the very first one on page 140. Each time he found a word in sequence that conveyed part of the message, he wrote down the number of that word from one to so on.

The message that would be sent via telex to Rome read:

Dear Aunt Seraphina:
Received your cable of the 15th. Sorry I can't make it on the 20th or the 25th. Hope the 29th will be all right. Expecting 45 to 60 people at party. Please arrange food for at least 75.

By the way, my new address is not 1041, but 1114. Send bill there, but try to keep cost to 2000 pounds, not over 3000 per person. Recipes I would like you to use are 4112 and 5516 in your book.

Love, Lenore

By using the number to lift words from the novel, the decoded message would read: SITUATION PARTIAL. RISK STILL FACTOR DUE TO UNKNOWNS. SUGGEST FIRST CHANCE REMOVAL.

Carter was pretty sure they wouldn't risk going on beyond Istanbul.

He picked up the copy of the Rome Telex and headed

for the woman's stateroom. He used the key he had taken from Lundesburg.

The bathroom door was open and she was just stepping from the tub.

"Damn, the least you could do is knock!"

"Get dressed," Carter said curtly.

"Rome." Her lower lip was curling.

"That's right."

It was almost eight. The telex had been sent to Rome four hours earlier. Since then, 121 telexes had been received for the passengers in the small room adjoining the big communications center of the ship. Carter had pored over the names and content of every one of them.

So far, no luck.

The third officer on duty was named Colby. He was young, probably under thirty, but he had a wise, careful look, and according to the captain, he was a man who could keep his mouth shut.

So far he had, making no comment about a passenger being in Com-Center, let alone that passenger reading every private incoming telex and okaying each one's delivery.

"More tea, sir?"

"No, thanks," Carter said, rubbing his eyes. "I think my liver's all Tannic acid now. I'm going to hit the head again. Don't—"

The machine buzzed and then stared clicking. Colby slid across the floor on his rollered chair and glanced down as the high-speed printer went to work.

"Rome?" Carter asked. It was the question he had asked fifty times in the last hour.

"No, sir, London." Carter had his hand on the knob, when Colby spoke again. "It's for a Monica Sims."

In four steps Carter was behind him, reading over his shoulder.

MONICA SIMS
PASSENGER
NOMAD SHIP GRECIAN MIST
AT SEA
TEXT: WILL MEET YOU ISTANBUL

Before Colby could reach forward, Carter's hand had ripped the sheet from the machine.

"This one you don't log, son."

"But, sir . . ."

"No log."

"Yes, sir."

Carter carefully folded the message and placed it in an envelope. "Call a steward and have it delivered. When that's done, you can call your relief."

"Yes, sir."

Carter went down six decks and along a passageway to the infirmary. He rapped once and Sylvia Leibstrum, starchy in a nurse's uniform, opened the door. Carter slipped inside.

Ellis, his face a road map of worry, sat at his desk trying to get a trembling cup of coffee to his lips.

Carter guided Sylvia by an elbow to the far end of the room. "How is he?"

"Shaky, but I think he'll pull it off. You got an answer?"

Carter nodded. "Remember what I told you about my friend Pierre Leduc in Tangier, his fantastic memory?"

Her shoulders sagged as the tension went out of her body. "Your hunch on the university records."

"That's it," Carter replied. "Monica Sims's phenomenal

photographic memory. That's where all the notes on the meetings are stored. I'll bet anything on it."

"But that doesn't make it foolproof, does it? I mean, that she's Volga?"

Carter turned and glanced at the lightboard above Ellis's desk. There was a tiny light on a ship layout that came on for the corresponding stateroom whenever the phone in the stateroom rang the infirmary.

"We'll know soon enough," Carter said. "Do you have the two splits?"

Sylvia held up two small bottles of champagne. "The one with the little peel on the corner of the label is the doctored one . . . literally."

EIGHTEEN

Hallam Dalton sat morosely in a chair smoking a thin cigar. He didn't want to be here. He was thinking about the tall redhead in Stateroom C-12. Last night she had played games. Tonight she had practically begged him.

So where was he? In Monica Sims's stateroom.

Damn the woman. There was hardly anything but business between them anymore. In fact, they hadn't slept together for over a month. Her function was to memorize, record in that phenomenal mind of hers.

Why had he ever told the others she had this capacity? They had jumped on it: nothing would ever have to be written down.

"You look unhappy, darling."

"I'm rather tired," Dalton replied. "And you said you weren't feeling well at dinner."

She was behind the bar holding a bottle of champagne. She freed the cork from the wires and popped it out. She poured two glasses. Then she took a small packet from her purse and poured the contents into one of the glasses.

"What's that?" he asked.

"Something to settle my stomach." She started toward him. "I want you to stay with me tonight, Hallam. I'm lonely, and I haven't been feeling well, really."

Swell, Dalton thought, taking the glass from her hand, *you don't feel well, so I have to stay celibate tonight!*

"Cheers."

She drank the glass in one swallow. Dalton took a sip of his and set it down. "Really, Monica, if you don't feel well, I think you should rest."

He started to rise. Gently, she pushed him back into the chair. Then she started removing her clothes.

There was not much to take off. The shoes, the skirt, the blouse, pantyhose . . . and there she was. Full breasts pouted proudly, buttocks and hips beautifully curved. Her arms were strong, her legs were long, and her body, like a shimmering sculpture, was absolutely devoid of hair.

Sitting in the chair, Dalton felt a surge in his loins. She was being erotically kinky, the way she'd been when they first met. He had thought, by her coldness lately, that she had forgotten all the things he liked.

"Do you still want to go, darling?" she purred.

"No," Dalton rasped, his throat dry.

She made a small, formal bow and walked back behind the bar. Unseen to him, she carefully washed out the glass and then poured it full of champagne. She came back to him carrying the bottle.

"Tonight, Hallam, I am going to show you how much I appreciate everything you've done for me. Drink, relax, I'll be right back."

In the bathroom, she checked her watch. With two glasses of champagne to activate the drug, it should take about forty minutes. She would make sure he stayed that long.

She flipped the taps on the tub.

In the sitting room, Dalton was getting impatient. Maybe it was all an act. He had begun to think that she was an act. She had been so erotic when he first met her, so wild, ready for anything. And then, once she was his secretary, it had become a once-in-a-while thing.

Where the hell was she?

When she returned he said somewhat curtly, "Did you take a nap or something?"

"Or something." Monica smiled. "I was drawing your tub, kind sir. And that massive tub takes a hell of a long time to draw."

The gleaming body rippled near. She made her little bow again, then took Dalton's glass out of his hand and set it aside.

Suddenly she clutched her chest and swayed.

"What is it? What's wrong?"

"Nothing," she smiled, "a little pain. I told you sometimes I get them. Come along."

She led him to the bedroom, helped him out of his clothes, and in the bathroom took him down the three steps into the enormous tub and got in with him. She let him repose for a while, soaking in the warm water, then she soaped him and washed him, tenderly.

Out of the tub she toweled him briskly, dried herself, took him to the bedroom, and gently hoisted him onto the bed. Dalton lay prone as her skilled fingers kneaded his muscles until all the fatigue was out of him, until he lay relaxed, contented. And only then did her hands relinquish their labors and her tongue went to work.

No more hands. Only the consummate art of the licking tongue.

It started at the nape of his neck, and then across his shoulders and under his armpits, then slowly down along his spine. Dalton took it as long as he could, groaning his erotic delight. Finally he turned.

"Don't stop . . . good God, Monica, don't stop!"

But she had stopped. She was on her knees, her face white, and she seemed to be gasping for air.

"Monica, what is it?" He touched her. Her skin was on fire.

"Pain," she gasped, "here . . ."

And then she toppled over

According to Ellis it was a slow night, with only a few minor emergencies to take care of. A woman had called complaining that her poodle had indigestion; she couldn't understand why the ship's doctor couldn't prescribe for animals. According to the woman, her poodle wasn't really an animal. A drunk had reeled off a barstool in one of the lounges and cracked his head. Sylvia had accompanied the doctor on that one, explaining to crew members who wondered that she was just doing public relations. And one of the busboys had popped in minutes before with a cut hand.

Now it was nearly midnight, and Carter was growing fidgety. Maybe Monica Sims wasn't going to take the bait. Maybe the cable to Rome hadn't been strong enough.

Or, worst of all, maybe Monica Sims wasn't Volga after all.

He pushed that thought from his mind and opened his cigarette case.

It was empty.

He cursed and again glanced at the big round clock on the wall.

"Don't worry," Sylvia said, "it will happen. I've got the ESP, I can feel it." She tapped the side of her head for emphasis.

And then it did happen. The light above the number for Monica Sims's stateroom glowed red.

Carter placed his hand on one phone and nodded to Ellis across the desk. The man's hands were shaking and his lower jaw quivered. His face glistened with sweat.

"Pull yourself together, Ellis," Carter growled. "Pick it up."

"In . . . Infirmary, Dr. Ellis, speaking."

"Doctor, this is Hallam Dalton. I am in my secretary's stateroom, sky deck four—"

"Yes, Mr. Dalton, calm down. What's the problem?"

There were a few strange squeals from Dalton's agitated throat, and then he again managed words. "It's my secretary. She just keeled over and now she doesn't seem to be able to get her breath. And her body is burning up!"

"I'll be right there."

Ellis and Carter replaced the phones simultaneously.

"Let's go," Carter said.

"God, I . . . I can't . . ."

Carter yanked him out of the chair by the lapels if his jacket. "The hell you can't. Grab your bag . . . move!"

Carter stayed in the passageway, pacing and smoking. It would be up to Sylvia to make sure Ellis performed.

Inside the stateroom, they found Monica Sims nude on the bed. Dalton was struck dumb at the bar, a freshly poured glass of brandy in his hand. He was fully dressed.

"She was just about to take a bath. I was in here, I heard her fall, and ran in."

"If you'll just wait here, sir," Sylvia said, and joined Ellis in the bedroom, closing the door behind her.

The doctor was already going through the motions . . . stethoscope, pulse rate, pupils. . . .

"Well?" Sylvia asked.

"All the signs are there."

"Then what the hell are you waiting for?"

Swallowing and wiping the perspiration from his face with a sleeve, Ellis opened his bag. He extracted a hypodermic and a rubber-tipped vial from Reisling's small black case. Two tries and he couldn't hit the rubber tip with the needle.

His hands were useless to him.

"Give me that thing," Sylvia hissed, snatching the needle and the vial from Ellis before he dropped them. "How much?" she said, holding them up to the light.

"Two c.c.'s. Be careful . . . no more."

Carefully, Sylvia slid the plunger back, pulling two c.c.'s of fluid into the glass tube.

"All right, where?"

"Turn her over."

Sylvia did. "Now what?"

"In the crease of the buttock, there. Check for an air bubble."

Sylvia did, and then eased the needle into the woman's body in the crease between her soft buttocks and her thigh. When all the fluid was injected, she withdrew the needle and returned it and the vial to the small black case. The case she slid into the pocket of the white uniform.

Ellis had gotten some of his faculties back. He was turning the body back over and re-examining the woman.

"It's already starting. The vital signs are diminishing."

"How long?" Sylvia asked.

"I don't know, for God sake!" Ellis snapped. "I've never simulated death before!"

"How long do you guess, dammit?"

"Somewhere between five and ten minutes."

They were an eternity passing, with Ellis monitoring the progress every few seconds. At last he flopped into a bedside chair, bathed in sweat, and nodded.

"All right, you stay here," Sylvia ordered. "Lock the door behind me. I'll get rid of Dalton and get the gurney. Don't let anyone in, you understand?"

"I understand," Ellis nodded weakly. "Oh, God, this is awful . . ."

"Just do as you're told."

Sylvia half dragged him to the door. She slipped through and waited until she heard the lock click behind her.

Hallam Dalton was still at the bar nursing his drink, his eyes wide. "How is she?"

"Mr. Dalton, I'm afraid Miss Sims is gone."

"What? Gone? What do you mean, *gone?*"

"Your secretary is dead, Mr. Dalton. The doctor is guessing cardiac arrest. Did Miss Sims have any history of heart trouble?"

"I . . . oh, God, I don't know. She complained of pains . . . *dead?*"

"I'm afraid so."

"What a mess. Months of work, this trip down the drain . . ."

You prick, Sylvia thought, but she managed to keep a straight face. "Where is your cabin, Mr. Dalton?"

"Uh, next door. I have the adjoining stateroom."

"I suggest you go there. The doctor and I will do everything in here. The captain will have to be informed. He will need a great deal of information from you."

"Yes, yes, of course."

She saw him through the connecting door, and moved to the passageway door. Carter met her at the stairs.

"It's done."

"Ellis?"

"He's shaky, but holding up pretty well." Sylvia handed him the black case, which he slid into his inside jacket pocket. "I'm getting the gurney."

"Give me at least an hour for the stuff to take effect." She nodded. "What about Dalton?"

"He's bearing up well," she said dryly. "More worried about what's in her head than the fact that she's dead."

"He's the type," Carter growled.

* * *

This time Carter didn't use the key. He tapped on the door with one of the bottles. It was opened immediately.

"I thought," she said, "that you weren't coming."

He moved past her into the stateroom. "Last-minute details."

She closed the door and moved with him to the center of the room. She looked good in a print sundress. Hard points stressed the sundress on either side where her nipples thrust against the material.

"It's done," Carter said, and saw the shiver that went through her body. Lenore Bonstedt, he thought, made a lousy spy. "And I heard from Washington."

Her head came up, her eyes alive. "About me?"

He nodded. "All good news. You'll go off in Istanbul with us. A few weeks debriefing, and you'll be on your own with a new identity."

"And money?"

"All you'll need," Carter said. "I told you, cooperate with me and I would take care of you."

The shoulders sagged and obvious relief spread across her face.

He held up the two splits of champange. "We'll celebrate."

Without waiting for a reply, he moved to the bar and popped the cork. Carefully he poured, the bottle with the torn label in his left hand.

"To your new life," he said, passing her the glass in his left hand.

"Thank you," Lenore replied, and drank, greedily.

For the next twenty minutes he watched her finish the split of doped champagne as he spun a tale of the good life she was going to lead in the West.

The combination of relief and champagne made her girlish and giddy. She slid onto his lap. Her skirt hitched up and he saw all of her slim and sensuously curved legs. Her hair spilled across his face as she brushed his lips with hers.

"I've really been trained to do only one thing, but I am very good at it," she murmured.

Carter smiled. "I'll just bet you are."

"Let me show you my gratitude," Lenore whispered, running the tip of her tongue along his lower lip. "You won't regret it."

"We have time, lots of time," he said. "Finish your champagne."

For the next half hour he held her off. Then it started hitting her. First it was perspiration, then dizziness.

"I . . . I don't know what's wrong with me . . ."

"Maybe the champagne," he offered.

"Yes, yes, that's probably it. No dinner . . ." She swayed against him.

"Maybe you should lie down."

She could only nod. Her breath was coming in gasps now. His face was swimming before her eyes, but she could see the lopsided grin.

And then she knew.

"Bastard . . . you bastard . . ."

He caught her before she hit the floor, and laid her on the couch.

Ten minutes later he answered the knock on the door.

Sylvia, followed by the doctor, wheeled the gurney into the stateroom. There were no words; none were needed. Carter had verbally rehearsed this with the two of them several times.

He handed the black case to Ellis, and picked Monica Sims up and carried her into the bedroom. He laid her across the bed, and Sylvia immediately went to work dressing her.

Back in the sitting room, Carter and Ellis lifted Lenore Bonstedt onto the gurney.

The doctor was calm now. There was only a little shake in his hands as he administered the injection. He replaced everything in the case and handed it back to Carter.

Sylvia reentered the room. "She's dressed." She handed Carter a white card. "That's her national insurance card. I took it from her purse. Next of kin is an uncle in Surrey, Howard Sims."

"I'll just bet uncle," Carter said, pocketing the card.

In the passageway, they turned left toward the special elevator that would take them and the gurney below to the infirmary.

Carter went up the steps. On the quarterdeck, he moved forward toward the captain's office and stateroom. The captain had already been briefed. Chances were he already had the telex prepared for the Bristish consulate in Istanbul. All he would have to do now is send another telex to the next of kin, the "uncle" in Surrey. It was ten to one that Howard Sims was already waiting in Istanbul.

Amidships, Carter paused at the rail and threw the thin black case as far as he could. When it disappeared into the foam, he continued on, checking his watch.

They were due to dock in Istanbul in three hours.

NINETEEN

Carter stood at the rail, watching the gurney being wheeled from the baggage bay of the ship onto the pier. The ship's first officer, Dr. Ellis, and Sylvia followed the two attendants.

The body was slid into the back of the ambulance and the doors closed.

Papers were signed and exchanged. The ambulance drove away, and the three people moved back into the baggage bay.

Carter lit a cigarette and watched until the ambulance was out of sight. Then, with a smile, he moved forward to the boat deck restaurant.

"Just coffee for now, please."

Before him, the high window-wall framed a beautiful view: the Bosporus winding north to the Black Sea, with the morning sun spreading across the rolling countryside of the Rumeli Hissar on the near side and the Anadolu Hissar on the far side. Both country and water gave off a soft golden haze.

Sylvia slid into the opposite chair and poured coffee from the half-full pot the waiter had left.

"Any problem?" he asked.

"None," she replied in a low voice. "Little Lenore is on her way to the basement of the British consulate."

"And from there, I'll bet right on her way to Moscow."

They both ate a leisurely breakfast. They were on cigarettes and coffee when the waiter approached the table. He plugged a jack into a socket and handed a telephone to Carter.

185

"Thank you."

The Killmaster waited until the waiter was out of ear-shot, and lifted the phone. "Yes?"

"Mr. Stevens?"

"This is Stevens."

"This is Glaston at the British consulate. The uncle picked up the package about twenty minutes ago."

"Was he followed?"

"Of course. It was a rented ambulance. It drove directly to Yesil Koy Airport."

Carter smiled and checked his watch. It was nearly eleven. "And the flight schedule I mentioned?"

"There is an Aeroflot direct to Moscow departing at noon."

"Thank you."

Carter hung up and held his hand out to Sylvia. "It's time to finish it off."

They talked as they moved belowdecks.

"What about Ellis?" she asked.

"He'll discover by Athens that I'm no longer on board."

"And he'll run."

Carter nodded. "It's just a question of who gets him first. But don't pity him."

"I don't," she said. "He brought it on himself."

They had just reached the sky deck, when Hallam Dalton passed them without looking up. He was flanked by two very stern, very large men in dark suits. Each one of the men carried one of Dalton's bags.

"MI6?" Sylvia asked.

"Yes," Carter said. "The rest of them will probably be taken to their various embassies by the end of the day. Their little trip is over."

"What will happen to them?"

"Not much, I would think. They will be interrogated, probably get a good slap on the wrists. They really weren't guilty of anything other than being naïve and stupid."

Carter used the key to let himself into the stateroom. A wheelchair was in the middle of the sitting room. He wheeled it into the bedroom. Together, they got Monica Sims into it and arranged a robe around her legs and a thick shawl around her shoulders. Sylvia tied a large scarf around the woman's head and arranged it so that very little of her face was showing.

Then they very carefully packed Lenore Bonstedt's two suitcases. Carter carried them while Sylvia pushed the wheelchair.

They used the elevator to go down to the seven deck on the harbor side of the *Grecian Mist*, away from the pier. The captain's launch was bobbing at the foot of the ladder.

Captain Walters himself stood at the top of the ladder.

"Your boatswain know where to take us?" Carter asked.

"Definitely."

Carter held out his hand. "Thank you, Captain."

"For what?" the man replied.

"That's right, Captain," Carter said with a grin, "for nothing."

Carter carried the woman down the ladder and settled her in straps in the tiny salon. He sat on one side, Sylvia on the other.

Seconds later, they were roaring across the bay.

Carter dropped his cigarette onto the tarmac and ground it out beneath his heel.

At the far end of the runway, the big C-101 turned for takeoff. The eight engines roared and then it was moving, lumbering down the runway. At last it lifted. The landing gear was swallowed up into the belly and the plane disappeared in the sun.

"What will happen to her?" Sylvia asked.

"You're just full of what-will-happen questions, aren't you?"

She shrugged. "I just don't like loose ends. Well?"

"You really don't want to know."

Carter opened the door of the limousine and handed her in. He joined her and leaned forward toward the driver.

"Yesil Koy," he said, and settled back into the seat. "Do you enjoy walking in the mountains, Sylvia?"

"I love it."

"Good," Carter said, "how about a little vacation in Switzerland?"

She snuggled into his arm. "I love Switzerland."

"Good. But first we have a little errand to do in Vienna."

The sounds and scents of the city seemed to bathe them as the taxi moved through Vienna. The area grew older and tougher as they neared the narrow lane of Borse Strasse. It was early evening and the whores were out in pairs, strutting in the minimal clothing they had to wear to show their stuff.

"Mmm, nice neighborhood," Sylvia commented.

"Refugee area, very poor," Carter said. "This is it, driver."

The cab pulled to the curb. Carter got out.

"Mind if I go in?" Sylvia asked.

"Suit yourself," he said, and dropped a bill on the front seat. "Wait for us."

As Carter and Sylvia emerged from the taxi, a woman came out of the door to the stairs. She looked rather slatternly in a garish wrapper. Her spongy face was disastrously powdered and rouged, and she had suspicious little eyes.

She acted as if she would bar their way, until Carter scowled. Then she moved aside and waddled off down the street.

The hallway was dark. Carter had to use his lighter to read the name plates on the mailboxes.

"Number three," he said, and they climbed the stairs.

Paint was peeling off the door and faint music could be heard from the other side. Carter knocked gently and it was opened at once.

Before them stood a dark, slim woman wearing slippers jeans, and a khaki shirt. Her long hair was prematurely graying, pulled back and tied with a ribbon. Her dark, luminous eyes were alert and questioning . . . cautious but not intimidated.

"Yes?"

"Alexis Brondosky?"

"Yes."

"My name is Carter, this is Miss Liebstrum."

"You are not Austrian, I can tell."

"No."

At one time she was probably quite beautiful in a soft way. Now there were lines of worry around her mouth and eyes.

"My papers are in order. Why do you harass me . . ."

"Frau Brondosky, we're not from the government. We have a mutual friend."

"Who?"

"May we step in? I don't want to discuss this in the hall."

She hesitated, but finally turned aside.

The flat was one room, two corners taken up with beds, another with a makeshift kitchen, and the fourth a seating area. Sitting primly on the couch, side by side, were two beautiful young girls.

Carter couldn't suppress a smile. The resemblance was striking. They had definitely gotten their father's hair and handsome features.

"Hello," Carter said.

"How do you do?" they said as one.

"I am Lara . . ."

". . . and I am Mira."

"My daughters. Please sit. I have no beer. Would you like tea?"

"No, nothing," Carter said. "We don't have much time, I'm afraid."

"As you wish. Who is this mutual friend you referred to?" she asked.

"A man, Frau Brondosky, who has made you a very wealthy woman. His name was Viktor Prokudin . . ."

DON'T MISS THE NEXT NEW
NICK CARTER SPY THRILLER

BLACK SEA BLOODBATH

The Spetsnaz camp was primitive but efficiently set up. The only fault Carter could find with it was the way specialists stuck together. Small groups sat together around their fires, their tents pitched nearby. Carter estimated that half of them were on patrol or guarding the science building.

He made a soft probe of the perimeter. Guards were set out at regular intervals. The Killmaster had to infiltrate, zero in on his targets, kill them, dispose of their bodies, and get the hell out.

By the time he had circled the perimeter, Carter had formulated his plan. He would hit the two communications men first; they looked like the easiest. He decided that the demolitions men seemed to be the toughest targets; he would need a Spetsnaz uniform to get close to them. The ones with the transmitters were holed up in a cave by themselves. The Killmaster knew they had made a bad choice.

Carter crawled past the outposts, skirting the sentries by only a few feet. At the mouth of the cave, he stopped, peeled Pierre from his inner thigh, and held the small bomb in his right hand. He crawled to the mouth of the cave, turned the two halves of the bomb, held his breath, and tossed the bomb between the two Spetsnaz.

They looked up, surprised, and then down at their feet where the two halves of the bomb were still spinning on the flat rock. One grabbed at his throat and crumpled to the ground. The other still had breath in his lungs. He started to go for his gun but was unable to hold his breath long enough to complete the maneuver. The P6 pistol dropped from his fingers and clattered down the rock leading from the cave.

A hand curled around the side of the cave and scooped up the gun. Carter waited. No one below in the camp made a move toward the cave.

He waited a minute before he went in. The relative openness of the cave had carried the gas away but not before it had done its job.

Out of sight of the camp he stripped the two bodies, then dumped them at the back of the cave. He destroyed their communicators, the red cylinders Nadya had described.

One of the uniforms was a perfect fit, the other small enough for Nadya to use. The Spetsnaz men were picked for size and strength. This one must have been one hell of a radioman, Carter thought. With difficulty, he put on both uniforms, one over the other.

It was time to move out again. The easiest way to get from point A to point B was to stop and talk with each group as they passed, accept cigarettes, and take a swig of vodka.

It seemed that the Spetsnaz were not very different from their army brothers worldwide. Bottles of the fiery liquid were everywhere. Obviously the General Secretary's edict of forced sobriety wasn't working here.

The demolitions men were off to themselves at the perimeter of the camp. Sentries walked their posts not twenty yards from them. Others sat at their campfires.

Carter knew he would have to hide their bodies in their own demolition chamber. Somehow he had to get to them separately, disable them, and stuff them in their trailer.

He joined them for a smoke. One was a man about his size, the other a few pounds heavier. "Another boring assignment, comrades," he said.

"As usual," the larger of the two said. He was sitting on Carter's right. The other was across the fire. All three were out of sight of the rest of the camp.

This was a tricky situation; he knew. These two were skilled killers. They were demolitions experts, but first and foremost they were killers. It didn't help that a score of Spetsnaz like them sat at campfires within earshot or that someone could find the dead men in the cave at any moment.

It would have to be quick and it would have to be silent. When he went for one, the other would react like a coiled spring.

He pulled a cigarette from a crushed pack in his borrowed tunic. The blazing embers that flared in front of him were all too big to use as a lighter. "Got a light?" he asked the man beside him.

As the big man leaned close, cupping a match in his hands, the flames partly hid him from his partner. The Killmaster grasped his tunic with his right hand and slipped Hugo between his ribs in one fluid motion. While the man died, he was held erect for a second or two as Carter readied himself for an attack.

He couldn't let him slip into the fire. Any outroar from his partner would be heard. The whole thing had to seem normal.

"What's the matter with him?" Carter asked, still holding the man erect, bunching his tunic in his left fist, the stiletto behind the man's back. "Is he sick or what?"

"What the hell you talking about? He's never sick . . ." the demolitions man said as he scrambled around the campfire. This was his camp. He had been sitting with his partner. Everyone here was Spetsnaz.

He was halfway through the sentence and leaning over his friend when the blade found his heart. It was a killing thrust. Like his friend, not a word was formed by his lips as the blood drained from his heart to flood his upper torso before the muscle stopped pumping.

It had all been so easy up to now. Four of the deadliest fighters alive had given up theirs lives without a sound. Carter knew it wouldn't all be this easy. His next move was to pile them in the demolition chamber and pull it out of there.

Carter dumped the bodies in the chamber, a steel-reinforced box on a trailer usually pulled by a four-wheel-drive vehicle. The box was used to detonate bombs the team couldn't defuse.

"What's going on here?" A sergeant appeared out of the gloom as the bodies disappeared.

Carter froze in the act of closing the lid.

"You know how it is, Sergeant," the Killmaster said as a could sweat broke out beneath his uniforms. "The colonel wants to show off our equipment to the local guy. That other colonel, the one with the hat."

"At night?" the sergeant asked suspiciously. "Nobody told me."

"So what else is new, comrade? They tell you everything?" Carter asked, regaining his cool.

"Sounds like you guys got yours at last," the sergeant said with a laugh. "You smart-ass demolition bastards got it easy. Where's your partner?"

"Taking a leak. Be back in a minute."

"Maybe a little extra duty's just what you need," the sergeant said as he moved off to another campfire.

Carter sauntered to the truck and backed it up. He had to get out and couple the trailer to the hitch with a dozen pairs of eyes on him. Finally he drove off through the sentry lines and around to the other side of the camp.

He left the truck behind a rocky outcropping where a few moonbeams sneaking through the cloud cover bathed the scene in light. No one would find it unless they were looking for it.

He was taking the whole operation one step at a time and with great care. For the Killmaster, his assignment was to destroy the science building and the tapes. He couldn't do that if he was dead.

Carter was walking up Nesterov Boulevard on the west side of Red Square when the men were found in the cave. He was too far away to hear the commotion the discovery created. He rounded the corner leading to Novaza Prospekt and saw the row of big old houses he'd seen before and catalogued in his mind. He could pick out KGB head-quarters. The communications building was located at the rear of the KGB building. He threaded this way through patrols of Spetsnaz troops and a few regulars hanging around their own headquarters.

"Got a light?" a Spetsnaz soldier asked. He was stand-ing behind a tree, guarding one of the big houses.

Carter reached for his lighter with one hand and snaked the Spetsnaz double-sided knife from its scabbard with the other.

While the enemy soldier took the light, Carter looked up and down the street. This one was too close to the action to leave as he was. No one was looking their way. He drove the knife up through the other man's diaphragm and shoved with all his strength, turning the blade, carving up the chambers of the Russian's heart. This was turning out to be a killing ground and it would get worse. He preferred subterfuge to outright killing, but he could play it either way.

He sat the body against the bole of the tree out of sight and wiped his knife on his camouflage pants. He walked slowly toward the KGB house and strolled past more troops unchallenged until he made it to the communications shack. He stopped in the shadows of the building and took two primed packages of C4 from his pack. With them in one arm and the AK-47 in the other, he kicked down the door and went in shooting.

Three men sat at a long table, hundreds of switches and a dozen consoles in front of them. They looked around in surprise and reached for hand weapons as Carter opened up. The 7.62mm slugs lifted them from their chairs and flung them against the monitors.

Carter set the timers on the two charges at ten seconds and positioned them against the incoming cables and the leads to discs on the roof. He ran from the shack yelling at the top of his lungs. "They're in the communications room! Get the bastards!"

Every soldier in sight rushed to the small building. Some made it inside. Others made it to the door only to be blown to fragments as the full force of the C4 blew.

Carter was curled behind a tree. Only one man nearby had survived. He was smaller than most of his fellows. He was looking at the American with hatred in his eyes, unslinging his rifle.

Carter got him in the throat with the projectile knife. The man looked surprised. The blade was stuck in his neck. Blood poured down his uniform. He tried to reach for the blade as his eyes began to glaze and his knees buckled. The man from AXE ran to him quickly, pulled off his boots and hat, then disappeared in the maze of new houses leading to the hills outside of town.

—From *Black Sea Bloodbath*
A New Nick Carter Spy Thriller
From Jove in December 1988

AMBUSH AT OSIRAK

A novel by
HERBERT CROWDER

Israeli forces are prepared to launch a devastating air
strike on the Iraqi nuclear production facility at Osirak.
Iraqi forces are fully aware of the oncoming attack. And
the Soviets have supplied them with the ultimate super-
weapon—the perfect means to wage nuclear war...